Blossoming Attraction

A Whimsical Dark Romance

Maebel Credence

Contents

Warning

Blossoming Attraction is a playfully dark erotic romance with an overly-imaginative heroine. This book involves fantasizing and events that include several themes that some readers may find disturbing.

Content includes: A large amount of smut, ravishment fantasies, consensual non-consent, domination, submission, capture, punishment, spankings, an alpha male.

Budding Attraction

Meet Cute

The job offer to place floral arrangements had been a dream come true. In this case, I just needed to transform the banquet hall of a century-old luxury hotel into a gothic-themed castle ballroom. And at ten thousand dollars, the contract was more money than I earned in five months. It also landed me on my first plane ride and into a big city. All I had to do was what I loved most—make a room magnificent.

After ten long hours of arranging the fragrant blooms, the place looked magnificent. With the job almost done, I'd earned a short *inspiration* break. And it was a break with the very novel that inspired the crimson and black roses that adorned every surface and climbed six feet up the thick pillars and stone walls.

I slumped onto a high-backed chair at a small, round table and pulled the book from my purse. As I opened the cover, I glanced past it to the two-foot by six-foot table that was blanketed with black and scarlet roses. It truly looked as though the dais in the novel had been brought to life—minus the heroine that would have been bound to it, of course.

The sight gave me reason to skip to the smut-filled pages I'd read many times. But as I was about to flip through, I caught sight of a six-foot-four man at the far end of the room. His fierce gaze locked onto mine for what felt like a brief eternity.

He resembled a clean-cut, early-thirties billionaire CEO type of antihero, or maybe a mafia king, but self-disguised as an average person in jeans and a fitted gray t-shirt.

In all my twenty-two years, no one ever looked at me with such intensity. More accurately, no one as handsome as him ever cast me a second glance.

Plenty of women passed through over the course of the day, but he gazed at me as though I were the only person in the room. Much like the billionaire in my smut-filled novel who'd captured a woman and bound her on the fictional table that inspired the dais in the center of this room.

These distracting thoughts wouldn't help me finish the job by evening. I needed an actual break, not to get heated at the thought of this man ravishing me on the rose-topped dais.

Shifting my attention to the book, I flipped through to the page where the antihero set up a trap to capture the heroine. That was a better start. Especially the way he stalked her from afar, every eerie moment heating her at the core.

My thoughts continued to dance between the words and the fantasy, blending the antihero on the page with the man across the room. And every time I wanted to look his way, a dip took hold in my stomach. The thought of him already caused me to blush a shade bolder than the crimson roses adorning the room.

A man slid the seat out on the left of me and sat as he said, "Good book."

It was the sort of *meet cute* moment that happened at the most inopportune time. The shame of my love of dark smut surfaced, reminding me of just how unacceptable people viewed it. Or maybe it was the way I'd been so enraptured by such a dark world that I lost awareness of my surroundings.

I glanced at a mid-twenties man whose black hair rested smoothly in a topknot.

Now my stomach churned with unease. Wanting to talk to a man in my mind was so very different from a real, in person conversation. The discussions in novels were hypnotic. The passion clearly shown with perfectly chosen words and conflicting emotions.

I swallowed, trying to find words after having been dragged from the imaginary world I loved to live in. "Thanks." I closed the book and slipped it into my purple handbag.

"It feels like we're there." He bobbed his head toward the center table, but watched me with a raised brow. "Especially the dais."

God, was he gorgeous with his neatly trimmed short beard and eyes that looked like a tropical sea of both green and blue. He was like a sun-kissed man from faraway islands. And he also knew exactly what inspired the dais that would easily become a bed of fragrant roses to bind someone to. To both punish and worship her for hours.

"It does," I replied. "I'm not done setting up the decorations, though."

I had little more to do, but I wanted the room to be absolutely perfect. And I needed to get away from him. Not that I couldn't imagine him dragging me over to the dais and using his belt to bind me to it. Even better, he would've come prepared with silk ribbon or smooth rope.

"Did you read Beca's most recent book?" he asked, relaxing in his seat and flashing a radiant smile that had my chest fluttering. His knowledge of this author, whose books I loved so much, made him even more heart-pounding.

I licked my lips, a bit embarrassed to admit to having read the romance that gave new meaning to *why choose* and vampire smut. "It was good."

The steamy romance novel was more than good. The two brothers played games of fire and ice, creating a world of opposites that were both agonizing and pleasurous.

"So, you liked it too." His head tilted back with a whimsical glance to the ceiling. "Which one did you like?" he asked. By the way he leaned closer with a teasing grin, I knew he was referring to which brother in the story excited me more.

"I..." my mouth felt as though cotton took hold. This seemed like baring my soul to an absolute stranger. A very handsome and charming one at that. "Why choose?" I asked, dodging the question.

He leaned closer conspiratorially. "I liked the sweet one."

"Right. Me too." I needed to get away before I revealed anything more about myself or said something to show him just how awkward I truly was.

Were I to be honest about his question, the sweet brother had his charms, but the dominating one who punished without mercy and forced pleasure just as cruelly made my pulse surge.

"I need to go." I had to hope my smile appeared friendly. The last thing I wanted to do would be to offend a guest at this lavish event, crushing all hopes of another opportunity to work at another grand occasion.

As I got up and walked away, I gave one last glance to the handsome man, whose grin could dazzle anyone. A man like him had to be the reason for every charming beta ever written.

But the other man across the banquet hall, whose stare was now accompanied by a scowl, was his own class of beast to be drooled over. The sort who certainly might have me strapped to a dais in inescapable bindings.

Masquerade

I expected my job would end before the masquerade began. I'd never designed at an event where I was required to remain. As it turned out, this job included me maintaining the bouquets and grand blooming displays throughout the night.

No matter how much I'd read about grand events where the wealthy bumped elbows or royals plotted against one another, I never experienced such a gathering.

I'd never branched out further than occasional trips across state lines. I had no reason to. Those events would have taken me away from my books or love of design. They would have thrown me into a world of people. Of conversation and awkward silences.

While speedily ushered from room to room with the servers who would work the grand ball, my dread mounted. But in a way, it did feel like I experienced the preparation to be in the presence of royalty. Like a renowned seamstress dressed me to be presented to my new groom I'd not yet met. Though, the way she rushed and fitted me with a black dress with far too much cleavage and a short ruffly skirt made it more like I was to be presented to be someone's chosen courtesan for a night. She cinched it tight with a crimson corset as bold as the flowers I'd meticulously placed.

The women to serve the event were dressed similarly, but with corsets of different shades. And very few of us had been fitted with black lace masks.

The mask at least provided me a bit of comfort in this setting of strangers, all with their own unique face coverings. Only a few of the men were of suitable age to imagine them being suitors who sought a worthy wife in a sea of corrupt politicians and espionage. And, though any reader knows such an event to only be fiction, this felt no less exciting than those dark romances filled with deception.

At the masquerade, I quietly wove through, caught between scouring for blooms that had been knocked astray or secretive men on the prowl, awaiting their opportunity to drag me into a shadowed corner. And given the masks of predatory creatures, I could easily assume I would become prey to a shifter who could undoubtedly bring me to complete submission.

As the crowd thickened, I was yet to see the tall man who'd stared at me as I worked during the day, but his forest-green stare remained burned into my eyelids. But equally curious for me to scout out and spy upon was the handsome beta with the vivid smile capable of calming any storm.

In this attire, and hidden behind a small lace mask and makeup that perfected my features, neither of the men would recognize me. Imagining what they might do would always be more enjoyable than an actual encounter.

I continued to look for them as I worked, attempting to remain as invisible as possible compared to the other women who flirted and batted their perfectly lined eyes. My efforts at going undetected seemed to work in this fantastical place that felt like the magical makings of an author. Like we were all people trapped in time. Dark and brooding lovers. Beasts in disguise. Danger of forbidden love and antiheroes in every shadow and corner.

When I arrived close to where chairs were in place for musicians to play, I stopped, taken aback by a couple who'd snuck into the shadows. I wasn't bothered that they were smashing the roses adorning the wide pillar. If anything, I felt a bit shocked. He had her wrists pinned over her head and her back to the vines and roses. At least they were thornless, but it still couldn't have been comfortable.

Oddly, she wore the same server dress and corset as me—minus a mask. Meaning she was a woman who delivered drinks or whatever small plates party-goers desired. She had higher ambitions that appeared to include snagging the heart of a wealthy man—no matter the risque behavior required in order to do so.

As the man lifted her thigh to his waist, a sole cello called out. It wasn't just a call for attention, but a declaration that came in the form of one of my favorite Elvis songs from my grandmother's record collection. *Fools Rush In*. No singer, only the cello.

I turned, spotting a man hidden behind a bronze wolf mask settled with the instrument between his knees. The music that rang out as he dragged the bow along the strings of the elegant instrument was more beautiful than I'd ever heard. The sort of music that could ground me into the moment, making the room beautiful in an inexplicable way.

Every step I took to the table that was only a few feet in front of him felt heavy. I wanted to stop. To simply look and listen. To melt into the music that made him so real.

When my fingertips were to the delicate petals of the roses, I glanced his direction. Even the way his fingers found their mark, mastering the strings, seemed visceral. Sensual, and with every single word of the song accompanying my awareness of his tune. Even Elvis's voice swirled into the music.

What a strange piece to be played at an event of this magnificence and scenery. But, somehow, it felt so right. Falling in love against all reason. In a themed world declaring it would be a most tormenting love, it will still be true love that would surpass where it had blossomed.

It wasn't until the enrapturing musical piece he performed ended and the musician rose I realized whose mastery of Elvis's most soul-capturing song set my heart ablaze. Standing at what had to be around six-foot-four and with eyes that flickered green from behind the brass wolf mask, this was the brooding antihero who'd watched me from afar. The man who'd craftily learned my soul over the course of time he'd studied my actions.

The realization terrified me without the music accompanying the sight of him. His face remained in my direction, giving me reason to flee into the ever-increasing crowd of strangers.

Work.

I needed to work. My imagination didn't need to stray. And work came with focus as more strings played, the beat tumultuous, and turning my surroundings into a dance floor of peril.

This music had an energy that matched the surrounding theme of jet black and scarlet. Of the danger from any direction and lurking behind any mask. Numerous women in my attire took their opportunity to dance, despite the possibility of what beast might linger behind the facial covering of their partner.

At five-nine, I was a woman above average height, but most of the men here weren't taller than me in the heels the seamstress supplied to me. Hiding required me to duck as I rearranged bouquets that were already misshapen after guests plucked them of the most beautiful blooms.

It didn't take long to see my antihero towering on the outskirts. But another equally tall man stood to his left, and his smile beamed like a beacon in the night. Pearly teeth set behind youthful lips I'd already heard speak. The man who'd loved my favorite author and read the same books I did. Whose conversation had me scurrying away—not that I wouldn't have fled a conversation anyway.

Two of them. Both with their upper faces hidden behind bronze wolf masks. One in his thirties and as clean-cut as an alphahole billionaire, and the other around mid-twenties who had silky black locks that flowed to his shoulders. A short, neat beard added to his look, making him a fierce but cuddly beta.

Now that I saw them standing beside each other, I knew they must have been brothers. The suits made them look like the sort of mafia heirs I could stay up all night reading about.

Given the way both masks landed in my direction, they'd come here to locate me. To capture me and drag me straight to the dais and bind me. Both of them doing the most wicked of things to me. Sure, that was only where my mind wandered, but I couldn't be blamed for enhancing this evening in a way that would have me lost in a fantasy wonderland for years to come.

I slipped behind a shadowed pillar, catching my breath in the snug corset. I'd had a silly conversation with the younger one. Only a discussion about a book with two brothers who captured a fiery heroine, one brother was fire, and the other was ice. Both were sexy as sin and capable of leaving a woman desperate to discover what would happen in the sequel.

My mind began to play on a loop. All the things the brothers in the story did were so blissfully tormenting. There may not have been a dais of roses in that particular book, but what would stop these two from finding me and dragging me to the one at the center of the dance floor?

They became the fantasy that shamelessly had me pinned down. One holding my wrists while I writhed beneath the other, whose tongue lapped at every inch of my body from my breasts to my aching core. Fangs sinking into me and injecting me with a saliva that made me desperate for blissful release.

I peeked the direction I'd last seen them, but they were no longer there. I questioned my own sanity as my heart raced in excitement for both of them. My curious study of the disguised guests soon landed on the older brother, who stood sentry at the large entry doors. He was amongst a group of men for the moment. But the slow lowering of his champagne fluke when his magnetic stare consumed mine made clear he'd discovered me.

Heat pooled between my legs. A heat that most definitely would have me drenched if I stared a moment longer. Quick, focused steps sped me from my hiding spot, and I wove between bodies. I could just find a new place to hide.

In my nervous rush, my shoulder bumped a woman as she was turning, causing me to mumble an apology for the clumsiness and hasten my steps. Nearing the musicians, I spotted the dazzlingly tall older brother's self-assured stride in my direction, setting his empty fluke on the tray of a passing server.

Breathe. Listen to the music. Focus.

Having failed to lose him, I tried my best to feign my interest in straightening a bouquet, letting the silk petals at my fingertips consume my senses. But, god, did the pulsing in my core increase as the male in my periphery closed in, too perfectly aligning with the conquering pace of the violin.

So steadily he approached that adrenaline increasingly pounded through me, but not quite causing a full panic. The danger, I knew, was only within my imagination. Yet, an exciting defeat added to the surrounding melody, leading me to imagine the glide of his hand along my back. Or maybe it had trailed over the tight corset fabric, creating shivers that reverberated deep in my bones.

"Dance with me." His voice proved as smooth as the bloom I held and as foreboding as the rapidity of the violin. At this nearness, when he stepped in front of me, his handsomeness outshined any sound or sight in the room.

My antihero. Both salvation and doom. I had no escape. No way to avoid this interaction.

A Dance

S everal seconds passed before my voice surfaced to respond to him. "I'm...um..." A swallow caught thick in my throat, choking any words that quickly fizzled in my mind.

He reached and guided my hand from the bloom that my trembling fingers no longer grasped. "You're going to dance with me." This time the words came out bolder; indisputably certain of his power to rule over my feeble will.

And by the way he assessed me, I had no doubt the look in my eyes answered any curiosity about whether or not he'd set a fire ablaze within me. They certainly promised him I wouldn't dare refuse his touch when his fingers laced into mine.

Yet again, I found myself lost in this crowd of unusual people. In muffled noise, drowning the violin's twisted satisfaction in whatever this stranger plotted to do to me.

The heeled shoes I wore felt akin to lead stilts as I followed him to the center of the banquet hall under the flickering candlelight of the golden chandelier.

Lightheadedness took hold, dizzying me. How does one even begin to dance? My conservative upbringing never permitted the crude behavior, so my experience committing such an unbecoming act could be counted on the fingers of my clammy hand he possessively clasped.

The excitement and fear surging within me gave an entirely new meaning to this darkly romantic opus that played. Luckily, it would end soon. I could thank him for the dance and excuse myself to return to my daydreaming of the dark and corrupt things the mysterious brothers would do to me. Or perhaps this dance would forever shape the outcome of every future floral creation as I let this fantasy blossom into a wicked darkness that would most certainly ruin me to the touch of any other man.

He pulled me against him. Closer than proper, but then again, propriety mattered little in this crowd that contained more than a few lecherous men who'd pulled women to the shadows.

After a clumsy landing of my foot, which didn't quite follow his backward step, he raised a curved forefinger to lift my chin, forcing my focus to his maddening emerald gaze. "Keep your eyes on mine." He enunciated those words in a way that hypnotized me into a desire to obey him.

"Yes," I breathed. My proper upbringing led me to add, "Sir." Or maybe it was the danger lingering within the tune. It seemed to declare that someone would be triumphant in this exchange, and I already knew it wouldn't be me.

His lips remained slightly parted as he swiftly moved left, leading me toward an abyss of darkness. Into the wicked shadows as the distant strings raced with passion. The rhythm couldn't possibly be so fast as it seemed if time dragged and my body became lost to the feel of his connection to me. And yet it seemed as though we became an integral piece to the violin as it raged, joining forces with others as it ascended into a crescendo.

The accompanying spin he set in motion as he unraveled me felt as though he planned to set me free if not for the glide of his hand on my forearm, which pulled me to him once again—to the erection that threatened of what might come of this night.

Couples flowed around us as he kept me close in an embrace that I knew wouldn't yield. Even when the music morphed into steady promises of too many looming possibilities of his triumph and my surrender.

"I'm going to fuck you." He spoke matter-of-factly; villainously husky and certainly possessive.

The warning pulled me from the fantasy that swore my doom at his hands. I believed his threat. Or was it a promise to fulfill a desire I didn't even let myself acknowledge? Either way, an involuntary quiver took hold of me.

If he did fuck me, as he claimed he would, it truly would be a night with no strings attached. One encounter that might break me at my core, given the size of his manhood bulging against my stomach.

If I were that type of woman, which, beyond dark fantasies and a vibrator, I wasn't.

I followed his lead as he moved backward. My footing proved even less graceful than when the dance began. How could I remain collected after the blunt warning of being fucked? And by a stranger whose voice dragged me out of the fantasy world I lived in.

His declaration continued, "I won't accept no for an answer."

While he assessed my responsiveness, the pads of his fingers dug into the corset and wandered downward to my rear, dragging as though talons might extend at any moment. The fear I couldn't hide must have excited him, because he added, "And you will fight me."

My shoes, that at one time felt like lead weight, seemed to morph into feathers as I succumbed to his guidance on the floor.

What more did I dream about than a man who would do just that? As though he'd been no more than a thought that became a reality for this evening. A man born to tease me into such a vulgar act.

"I'm going to rip your dress." He brought me closer to him, slamming me against the hardness at his groin. His possessive hold should have sent me running, but instead, it made me want his promises to come true. "And..."

Trepidation and desire burst forth in doses too strong for me to harness.

He spun us; the seconds dragging as I secretly bid the next promise to come.

"I'm going to bind your wrists."

The beat slowed, albeit more menacing with the cello's low wail.

His hand lifted mine to twirl me, this time returning me to him so that my back rested against his chest. His lips tickled my ear. "And you'll never escape."

He must have known the books I loved as well. Perhaps both he and his brother devoured the dark smut as much as I did. Making this blossoming encounter of ours all the more memorable.

He led me several steps backward, each more daunting than the last. Now his palm firmly moved down my corseted stomach, finding my core. The black fabric of the dress tucked between my legs, and I feared he might feel the moisture if he continued to stroke the thin material.

"I'll punish you without mercy if you try to get away," he added in a tone I found irresistible.

His mouth trailed down to my neck, the cold mask scraping as though nipping my sensitive skin as we turned as one being, slow and sensual as he floated me further into the darkened corner of the gothic banquet hall.

We'd become the conqueror and his prize, inseparable unless he willed otherwise. And, as the delectable encounter progressed, my terror built at the possibility that he might discover my shameful excitement. Not that I was the only one enamored and ready for a night of passion. The erection at my back had swelled to epic size.

Luckily, the wicked promises kept me at a loss for words. Nothing more than unadulterated honesty would spew out of my mouth, anyway, begging him to be the monster he tempted me with. Horns would most certainly extend upward as he morphed into a demon. Perhaps Satan himself had emerged to drag me down to the underworld, where he would eternally rule over my soul.

We spun into the darkness behind a pillar, further distancing me from the light.

He spoke again, this time even lower. "I'll ravish you every single day."

He could take me straight down to the depths of hell if such a fate awaited. I would welcome the doom; accept any bit of torment if it landed me in such a place with him. Fisting my nape, he gently pulled, tilting my face upward to catch the slight reflection in his turbulent eyes. He enunciated, "For–ev–er."

And he'd already instilled in me that the touch of any other man would never sate me. Ever. And those mesmerizing green eyes would plague my every fantasy and every book that would captivate me. Forever.

What went wrong in my life that those words could be so exhilarating? I'd been mostly well-behaved with men before this dance. Not that I'd spent time with many.

He'd shattered my inhibition and unleashed a primal desire within me to be his. For this dance to play out time and again, leading into a blackness no sane person dared to enter.

"Okay." I finally found my voice to breathe my acceptance. To let this passion occur in real life with a man I could only dream existed once I returned to my hometown of pitiful choices.

"Then you accept." His fist tightened into my long brown locks, forcing my mouth to angle ever upward. His lips crashed against mine. The intoxicating kiss most definitely staked his claim over my being. One that melted the world from around us and had the wicked possibilities bubbling inside me.

I'd be forcefully claimed by his beast, obedient to his every wish. My entire being would be his to rule over.

Even time became a tormentor as I awaited his next act that would deem me as his for the night. He pushed me forward against the rose-vined pillar, making me even more grateful they were thornless now that I was the one to be ravished against them.

I felt a few vines snap and yank from beneath my palms before he had both of my wrists in his hand and raised them above my head. Now I understood why the other woman so willingly let a stranger have his way with her. There was something magical about the smells and feel of the silky blooms against my cheek and chest that made this chance encounter even more delightful. Especially when he used the vines to bind my wrists above my head.

But what made it undeniably irresistible was the way the music changed, slowing to a calm and passionate piece. As though it answered to the moment, ruling over his beast to once again transform him into a man who wanted nothing more than to have me bound and at his mercy, yet gentle.

This time when his mouth grazed my neck, it felt nothing like my antihero, but like a man who knew all the ways to make a woman shudder from physical pleasure.

"You're so much more perfect than I imagined," he said low against my ear.

That was the way I felt about him. What I'd feared would be a dominating alphahole became my knight in shining armor. Dominant, but still caring.

His hand roved upward outside the corset, exploring my curves, coinciding with the cello's long cry that foretold my heart's unavoidable shattering to come before night's end.

Now I awaited the passion. In this blackness, with me bound inescapably, it could occur in so many ways. No one would know. No one else existed. I squeezed on the vines, aware of their fragility, wishing they were rope so I could completely let my being melt between this gorgeous stranger and the pillar.

He scrunched the short ruffled hem of the dress upward with steady grazes of his fingertips. Then came the strumming when he found my most sensitive spot, as though he'd turned my body into his beloved instrument. And I would gladly let him work his mesmerizing chords on me.

Intoxicated by this man's touch, I'd become lost to the bliss he elicited. Held captive by the lips that carefully kissed along the side of my neck. Enraptured by the awareness that he'd freed his cock and intended to use it on me, just as he'd warned.

In reality, though, STIs and pregnancy were a very real, life destroying possibility. Those annoyingly invasive thoughts always clawed me out of the moment of any good smut, and now they might ruin this encounter. I couldn't let one dumb decision forever destroy the rest of my life.

The words of refusal easily became trapped in my throat, wanting to vanish from thought. Especially when he ripped my thin thong. It seemed to have been designed for such an opportunity. Then came the glide of his engorged manhood, exploring my slit that didn't hide how much my being craved him.

"Condom?" I asked, already melting from the temptation I wanted to continue.

"No," he replied against my neck, rather curt.

Maybe this would play out like the book. This stranger could easily overpower me. If he wanted, he could force his hand over my mouth to silence me.

"I'm not on..." the size of his cock as the tip forced its way into me brought a pained gasp. "Birth control."

"Don't speak unless I give you permission to," he replied, continuing his endeavor to shove into me.

In all reality, I could simply walk away if he refused to listen to my demand for protection. He might have thought I was lying to him to continue the game of dubious consent that we both played. But I didn't want this to end, so I raised onto my toes, hindering his access.

"Do you have one in your room?" I breathed, hating how the words interrupted the moment.

"I warned you not to speak, Julie," he said, moving away from me.

I supposed he would easily have learned my name, but I didn't like the way he claimed to have warned me to be quiet.

This didn't go according to the deep hope of him ignoring my words while pursuing the sex he knew I wanted. I tugged at the vines that had secured me before a powerful smack landed on my backside.

I jumped forward against the pillar. *He'd spanked me!* And it hurt. Pain wasn't something I had the tolerance for, no matter what kind of dark romance books I read.

I yanked my wrists from the binding vines, but my attempt to free myself ended with him spinning me in his direction, pushing my back firmly against the wall and pinning my wrists above my head.

Reflections of light on his wolf mask and in his eyes offered a warning of a surfacing beast—of a cruel villain's rise. "I already warned you that you'd be severely punished if you tried to escape me."

Caleb

"It's my turn, John," another male voice said firmly. I recognized it as the younger brother. The man who'd so easily come to speak to me about the books I loved.

"She's disobedient," John quipped as his fingers found my slit. To me, he said, "I'm going to punish you for your bad behavior."

Oh, by god, I'd come between two unbelievably sexy brothers. But my backside still throbbed, making this far too real. The villainous brother of the two plunged his fingers into me, adding a different sensation.

John's other demanding hand landed on my chest and found my low neckline. He yanked, tearing the fabric and freeing a breast while he forced the corset downward. A pinch of my nipple between the knuckles of his long fingers jolted me with more terrified craving.

Unrealistic. This was the sort of unrealistic I might have rolled my eyes at. The on-page indecisive woman that I would want to stay with the man for the on-page smut, but also wonder why she was so insane not to escape what was certain to be a tension-filled nightmare to her.

And they planned to have turns with me, which made this encounter more than just the game I considered John to be playing.

I squirmed against John's hold. Even if this felt too perfect to miss out on, it wasn't worth actually suffering the pain and torment of whatever he may have had planned for my disobedience.

"*My. Turn,*" the younger growled.

I didn't know what to make of the encounter, but both disappointment and relief took hold of me when John freed me and stepped backward. I could get away, then go home and imagine this experience with my vibrator and dream up how this would have played out.

My spin for a quick retreat landed me against the younger brother's firm chest.

His long arm stretched upward to brace him against the pillar and block my path to freedom. I couldn't turn to rush into John's clutches, though.

"I need to be going," I said timidly, pulling my top into place. I certainly didn't need anyone else seducing me into foolishness in these shadows, even if he wouldn't cause me pain. His *turn* would end once he had his way with me.

"My brother, he..." the accompanying sigh made clear this was a frequent frustration regarding John. "He comes on a bit strong. How about we start over? I'm Caleb." He spoke as though starting over wasn't debatable.

"I really should attend to the decorations," I said, struggling to control the variation in my tone. I'd already begun to imagine this gorgeous, heart melting beta having his way with me. I could get carried away if I didn't remain strong and get myself out of this mess quickly.

"The fun part is about to begin," he said with amusement.

Just what exactly was his definition of fun? The way he said it added a reason for me to worry, but also a tinge of curiosity. Indecisive, yeah, I was all too aware of my flip-flopping the moment curiosity got the better of me.

"The fun part?" I asked.

"It's the part where you learn about everything we're going to do to you." As he spoke, the main area where people danced became brighter. The glow accented half of his shadowed face that was no longer masked, and I could somewhat see the handsome man's charming smile.

"Everything to do...to me?" I swallowed. Come to think of it, this had been a dark-themed mask. Gothic and gloomy, and I even felt dressed for some sort of frilly doom to happen to me.

His face came closer to mine. "All the different ways we're going to pleasure and torment the pretty little minx we purchased."

"Purchased, I..." I considered how many of the staff in the same attire seemed to have spent a lot of time dancing, amongst other non-work-related acts. "I'm not a prostitute."

Conflicting thoughts churned in my head. The older brother mentioned his obscene plans. They'd watched me all night and knew my name. And, unlike the unmasked people working the event, no one bothered me. As though none of the lecherous men were interested in me. Someone here had simply charged money for me to be a whore, and that hadn't been in the contract I signed as a florist.

My panicked thoughts on how to get out of this mess were shattered as he kissed me. But what knocked me to the moment was the end of the music. The place had gone absolutely silent, and the brighter lighting must have been meant for something. Parties don't go absolutely silent unless something sinister were to occur or just had occurred.

I twisted, creating a friction that had him grinding against me while his mouth remained on mine, and his tongue searched for weaknesses in my sealed lips. He even gripped me by the back of my head so I couldn't break free.

But this was all wrong. He'd claimed to have purchased me. Not purchase sex from me. Organized auctions and such purchases of sex from naïve women occurred in steamy books. And, if true and to be compared, whatever happened to someone sexually enslaved in real life wouldn't have the same passion as in dark romances. Real life was a horror compared to the worlds in the fiction I loved.

His kiss finally broke. "I kind of just want to fuck you instead of watching the show."

I had to think fast to escape a situation that was certain to end poorly for me. "There's a show...I want the show first." Let him trust me. Then I'd run. I already had a plane ticket, and the airport wasn't far. I could get there early and wait. I finally understood that this trip hadn't been about my decorating ability, so I wasn't hurting my reputation by leaving early.

"Whatever your heart desires." Caleb's grin appeared as wolfish as the mask he'd worn earlier. His hand took mine in a less controlling way than his brother had done. Hopefully, this would lower the handsome beta's guard. Though, in the book, the heroine didn't get away even when she gained the sweet brother's trust.

Sounds erupted, possibly slapping. We went into the light and wove through couples, but stopped beside a large pillar near the center. The stone table I'd so lovingly carpeted with black and scarlet roses now had a naked woman bent over it. But it wasn't how the book depicted a woman would be laid out on it.

If I could have turned and run, I would have.

Caleb grabbed my upper arms and pulled me backward against him, letting me feel just how excited he was at the sight of the old lecher thrusting into the woman, who barely looked twenty. I would have been screaming by the force he used, but aside from bobbing forward from every thrust, she remained motionless and quiet. Upon closer examination, though, her ankles had been cuffed and connected to the floor. Let's not bother with focusing on the way the old man held her forearms behind her back.

Had Caleb and John planned to use me that way? Absolutely not. But escaping his grip on my arms seemed impossible. I knew this wouldn't be a simple escape, especially when he was a loyal beta to an alphahole. I'd read about heroines attempting those irrational escapes that always ended in failure.

"We can go next." Caleb spoke as though it would be my privilege to be fucked in such a way.

I could hardly breathe as panic set in. That didn't stop me from feeling the hand that lowered to dig beneath the frilly skirt and cup my mound. And I knew I'd lost my mind when that touch had me aching for him to do more to me. But this wouldn't play out with me receiving countless orgasms or melting from the way his tongue would glide the length of my slit.

Louder slaps dragged me back to the moment. The old bald man's pounding increased to the speed that caused his mask to bounce from his head. Even then, it seemed as though the petite girl beneath him had become accustomed to this—as though it were a daily occurrence she'd grown used to.

I gasped with horror at what would become of me if I didn't escape the two no-longer-alluring brothers.

I would start out reasoning with him, so I wasn't in her position next. "You can have all the money I was paid to do the decorations." I pushed backward against his toned chest. "I can reimburse you whatever they took from you. I can give you extra. Just let me go."

"You don't have that much money." He purred the words against my hair. "Don't worry. I don't have to fuck you on the dais in front of everyone tonight if you want to wait a bit." His finger slid between my folds, exploring casually. "But I am about to find somewhere to fuck this tight little pussy until the sun rises."

I'd learned a few things for certain from movies and books. First, clever heroines can trick bad guys. Second, bad guys are always easy to seduce. Third...

I lost focus when he began to knead my left breast. It felt so much gentler than John. So dedicated to my comfort. So considerate of what pleasured me.

But Caleb was still a bad guy, hot though he might be. I needed to escape him, and not just after he'd knocked me up from an all night fuck-fest that would have me drunk on how good he felt.

At the dais, the old man released himself inside the bound woman. Immediately after, an even more geriatric man with saggy skin that juggled from his chin lined up behind her and freed his cock from his suit pants.

Caleb shuddered at the sight, too.

"We should probably go somewhere private," I said seductively, looking up over my shoulder at Caleb. I didn't have to fake the wanting tone in my voice, given how good his hand felt.

He hummed, leaning forward to kiss me. I wasn't so foolish as to refuse his mouth as it connected to mine. Successful escape required coaxing his ego, and, given the minimal effort it took for him to have my core hungry for release, that was easy to do.

His Long digits continued their dedicated pumps into me, but not rough like how the bound woman was currently being used. Unlike her careless abuser, Caleb responded to the swell of my every breath and the soft moans he elicited from me.

Why did he have to be a bad guy? He'd been so desirable. He still was, to the point that I wanted to ride out the pleasure of my submission—which only ever occurred in the darkest recesses of my hopelessly dirty mind. To be his for as long as he allowed.

But, in the end, that wouldn't play out to my survival. Torment would befall me if I continued to romanticize his ownership of me.

The more I writhed from the pleasurous touch, the faster his palm worked toward bringing my most sensitive spot to climax. If the hand to my breast and dedication to my slit weren't enough, the kiss that continued downward along my jaw and then to below my ear promised this would end too soon as my being came together in a crescendo of bliss.

The eruption sent sparks through me, competing with the fourth of July. Except this was no celebration of freedom. This was his triumphant win over my personhood.

My eyes fluttered with the rhythm of my tightening walls. This distraction from my goal to escape him, and my drunkenness on sexual attraction, was the downfall of any otherwise reasonable heroine.

Several seconds passed before my fuzzy mind remembered the only thing that mattered in this moment. *Get away from this man who just gave me an outstanding orgasm while amongst a bunch of rich elderly men who needed to pay to own someone in order to have sex.*

Departure

"**G**od, do I love you already," Caleb whispered.

His satisfaction with my orgasm proved to be in my favor. A man like him would be easily escapable.

"Come, sweet girl," he said, taking me by the hand again. Of the two brothers, he was by far the most charming. "We're going to go on a fun trip in a touring dungeon."

What millionaire has a mobile dungeon? Maybe all these rich creeps at this twisted event went from town to town to masquerade, fucking the women they rented or kidnapped. For the least I knew, there could even be a bunch of rich pervert mobile home parks.

The declaration proved he already had everything set in motion, including a mobile prison awaiting me outside.

No-fucking-thanks, kidnapper!

I had to school my reaction. I could make him believe I wanted to go on a trip in his torture chamber. I could master appearing obedient and willing.

"I knew you were the sort of girl to want to go on a little adventure." He turned, tugging me behind him as he speedily wove me through the elegantly dressed villains.

I kept pace. I just needed to get somewhere where I had the opportunity to run. Not as easy, but the best option since a dungeon awaited outside. Before we reached the massive red doors where I could escape, Caleb stopped abruptly, turning to catch me when I stumbled into him.

"I almost forgot..." His grin proved to be no less than devious, and his sea-green gaze seemed to dance. Before I could make sense of what he was doing, something soft landed on my right wrist. The smooth cuff he cinched on me felt nothing like the doom it meant for my life.

In all reality, he would have used metal or zip ties if he'd wanted to be cruel and terrifying. But almost all the drool-worthy billionaire alphaholes used luxury cuffs to ensure their prize couldn't escape.

As he found and secured the restraint, some of my favorite anti-heroes flashed into my mind, flooding me with euphoria. This captor's strong jaw and bold cheekbones outdid any man of my fantasies. As did the beaming grin that revealed his perfect teeth.

"We added your favorite color." Caleb pulled my other wrist forward and secured it as well.

When I inspected the black leather restraints with large metal buckles, they had a purple lining to the suede inner cushioning. It was my favorite color...but how did he even know anything so personal about me?

I fidgeted with the new imprisoning devices. "Thank you." Not that I appreciated the added difficulty to escaping, but the thoughtfulness was charming.

He snapped a tiny padlock on each of the cuffs, so I couldn't pry it off. "You are so very welcome, Julie." The way my name rolled off his tongue would make any sane girl want to be eternally obedient. Even worse, the way he reached up to cup my cheek resembled the touch of any prince charming.

But he was still a bad guy. Not the worst of the brothers, but a captor, no less.

My shift in thoughts caused a darkness to consume his expression. He must have caught my distrust. Captive women were to behave like little designer lap dogs, giddy for their Masters.

"I know what you're thinking, but you won't escape us," he said, lowering his hand from my cheek. If only I'd controlled my expression better. He wouldn't be pulling my hands behind my back and snapping the cuffs together. His tone went husky. "I promise I'll make sure it's fun for you every time you try."

That only had an unnatural amount of heat building within me at the memory of a few of my favorite scenes of failed escape. And Caleb wasn't like the alphaholes. He was the one who would let down his guard—especially since he believed these cuffs guaranteed I couldn't flee.

I nodded. "I know."

"Come on, beautiful." Caleb took a gentle hold to my forearm and led me forward.

Not a single person we passed considered us odd. Everyone here knew this lifestyle well. Slave and Master, with me seemingly well behaved.

We arrived at the double-doors, him nodding to two large men in suits before he opened the doors. They must have been there to keep the unwitting captives from escaping.

Once outside, we didn't need to walk but a few steps before I spotted John loading my small purple luggage into a black Toyota SUV.

A Toyota. Not a Porsche or Lamborghini, not even a BMW. A fucking Toyota.

That was when reality, untainted by fantasy, burned into my psyche.

I was probably the cheapest sale of the night. So much for a clever escape and then going home with the billionaire romance fantasy to play in my thoughts. They weren't even wealthy.

The older brother's scowl bore a predatory wrath that appeared hopeful that I would be dumb enough to attempt an escape.

He'd gotten me hot and bothered during our dance. Even created a need to be ravished in the shadows before he refused to consider wearing a condom.

No matter how much I wanted to ignore his handsomeness, I couldn't. I was still attracted to him, just less so, given the Toyota.

John didn't give me more than a glance before briskly getting into the driver's seat. Maybe he already struggled not to bend me over and relieve the pent-up tension from our sultry encounter in the shadows.

Caleb definitely seemed more kind and innocent, and my choice of who would keep watch over me. Luckily, he was the one to help me onto the back seat and scoot in beside me.

Music already played low on the speakers. The same ominous classic that warned of my doom as John and I had danced not very long ago.

I unwittingly sought the rearview mirror, catching the intense stare of his that landed on me. It didn't last long, thankfully, but my first dose of deep terror sank in. Not that I wasn't already concerned, but that man successfully saw to my capture and seemed ready to ensure it.

Caleb helped to place the middle seat belt over me, then the SUV slowly crawled out of the parking lot that was lined with luxury cars.

And I was getting hauled off in the only Toyota. I'd never considered myself conceited, but it ruined my self-confidence to know I'd been the cheap deal of the evening. Not exactly the heroine of a good story, just a country girl with a big imagination and very few life experiences. And as our journey continued, that truth of myself had me sulking while I watched the lights of buildings and other vehicles zoom by.

"Julie, sweetheart." Caleb's voice was husky, and his warm hand tickled up my outer thigh, roving beneath the ruffles of the dress.

"Don't coddle her," John snapped. "She's a slave. Not your girlfriend."

I didn't dare react to John's lack of sentiment.

"He gets grumpy after bedtime." The younger brother spoke too low to be heard over the tormenting classical piece that made the drive feel even more damning and inescapable.

If only this could play on fantasy again. Two sexy men taking me away to be theirs to mercilessly pleasure me. Welcoming me to a world that had always been out of my reach. Fucking me in a way I loved, but I would defiantly claim to hate.

If anything, focusing myself on that mindset would win their trust. It would ensure I had my chance to escape them when the perfect opportunity arose.

Billionaire alphahole, sunshine beta, merciless sex...

Toyota. There went that daydream. But something still wasn't right about all of this. These men must have infiltrated that event that had the uber wealthy creeps who were willing to own someone. It hadn't been a rescue mission, although that would have been fun, and left me indebted to them.

"How much did you pay for me?" I blurted the words.

Caleb shushed me, turning to have a better angle and fondle my left breast while planting his mouth against mine.

I wouldn't be silenced or distracted with pleasure, though.

Something about this felt too strange. The trickery, the ten thousand dollars, John the epitome of any controlled and sexy billionaire I'd ever read about.

Then came a middle-class, family-friendly Toyota. The dungeon would have been something to grasp my imagination. But that hadn't even been an actual vehicle.

I turned my cheek to Caleb. "And this *Toyota* isn't a millionaire sex dungeon."

The SUV swiftly pulled to the side of the road with a jerky stop that jolted me forward. One would think the vehicle had become offended by my statement. I may have been blunt, but I hadn't been so rude as to deserve that response from the almighty jerk driving.

He turned in his seat, absolutely infuriated by the lethal glower burning a hole into my soul. "Do you have a problem with this car?"

I could have sworn the music increased with his hostility. This now seemed like an inescapable dance between locked doors and the Toyota-driving alphahole.

I cowered, and my head shook nervously. "No problem."

"Complain again and I'll leash you to the back so you can jog to the airport." He jerked back into position to start the trip again.

Airport. We were going to the airport. I could safely escape the psychotic male who clearly took his Toyota's socioeconomic status a bit too personally. After that confrontation, we rode in a haunting quiet, dominated only by the impassioned instrumentals.

Backseat Bliss

I vaguely placed us about twenty minutes from the airport when Caleb kissed my neck, trailing downward. "Julie," he purred. Sex oozed from his tone. The sort of sound I loved to read about. A wooing.

I needed to respond with equal interest if I were to come out unscathed. We were about to be at an airport. He needed to trust me not to run from him.

"Yes," I answered. The way he unbuckled both of our seatbelts informed me of his intent to switch to an unlawful position in the moving vehicle.

"I need to fuck you." His words came out with a hum before his weight pressed me into the seat. And he was sexy enough to bring me to the moment.

A thousand yeses sloshed in my confused mind that was already littered with contradictions. Something horrible must have happened in my upbringing that had me shading this man so positively. Maybe the fact that I'd spent too much time alone.

I'd simply gone mad and didn't want the experience to end yet. This was a moment in which part of the fantasy could be experienced. There wasn't an opportunity for escape, but there was an opportunity to make my capture memorable.

"Okay." I replied as I had answered when John warned of demolishing my body with his massive cock. When his words of conquest filled me with lust. But all of this ended at the airport. I couldn't become pregnant with a captor's child moments before freedom.

"I could please you with my mouth," I said to the charming beta, all too eager to ride this rollercoaster a little longer.

"God yes!" he returned upright in his seat with his splayed hand already wrapping the back of my head.

"Hands." I twisted my joined wrists to my side. "I need my hands free to do it right." Not that I knew how to give a high-priced blow job, but unless he wanted to just hold my head in place, I needed to support myself and grip him as I took the massive length all the way to my throat.

He'd started to unfasten his suit trousers, but his efforts shifted to the bindings at my wrists, disconnecting them.

There were plenty of men at the masquerade who needed to pay to find a woman to do this. But Caleb? That seemed ridiculous to believe. Sure, he didn't travel in a Maserati, but he still had a high tier presence. The gorgeous man could probably get out of the car and hold out a sign that boldly declared he wanted a blow job, and women would get into wrecks pulling over to service him.

Once he separated the cuffs, I positioned myself to lean over his lap. Bracing one hand against the door, I pulled the zipper of his pants down with the other. I hadn't fully freed the girthy manhood before a gasp escaped him. Wrapping my fist around him and lowering my face, I took the velvety tip to my lips, opening slowly.

This would be the moment in a book when I rushed to make myself an espresso at home. The point in the story where things came together, be it romance, or a redeemable alphahole demanding to use my mouth as nothing more than a receptacle for his seed. It's the act of submission when the female's nonsensical thoughts pull her back and forth like a cloth doll. But now, sure, I could lie to myself and anyone else wanting me to fight this and escape without satisfying a villain's demands. Were I dealing with John, finding a way to get out of it or rush the act might seem more reasonable.

Caleb seemed genuinely caring. He wasn't the mastermind. But mostly, how many opportunities does a woman get to feel a man's responsive pleasure and know she alone brought it? Caleb's eyes were on me. His hand rested gently on my head. Not one moment of sucking his manhood felt degrading. Not a sensation felt disconcerting. If anything, I felt more alive.

"Oh, please, Jules," he moaned.

The moment didn't quite feel dark enough to my preferences. He'd even given me an affectionate pet name. No one had ever given me a pet name. He was my enemy, the one who knew how to torment me on a visceral level.

Come on, Caleb! Do a better job at being the villain I fantasize about until there's not a single vibrator in my home with a remaining charge. If this was going to happen, I damned sure wanted to think about it fondly for the rest of my life.

I may never have given someone else an order in my life, but I wouldn't let this attempt at enslaving me turn into a mundane memory. I grabbed the caring hand he slid over my shoulder and shoved it into my hair, forcing it into a fist at my nape. Not hard, of course. I still wanted this to be a positive memory once I snuggled safely in bed at home, contentedly alone.

Caleb's fist tightened and loosened around my hair, pulling and releasing with a sensation that hovered on minimal pain and incredible pleasure. Something about the squeezes caused me to move my head faster and pump the length of his cock as he let me know how much he loved the slow suction and twirling of my tongue.

All over again, I felt as though the devil had risen to claim me and drag me down to his underworld of gratification.

That feeling of divine sin grew the moment the fingertips of his free hand slid beneath the torn lace neckline of my dress, finding my nipple that already tingled from the euphoria of the experience. It probably provided him with too much excitement, because in moments, his hips jolted upward, roughly stabbing into my throat for the first time in this experience.

"Jules." Caleb's groan rolled out as the fist in my hair tightened to the point his hold stung. Hot bursts of seed pulsed into me, near gagging me until I had no choice but to swallow.

"We're in a bit of a hurry!" John snapped from the front, pulling me from the sexy moment with Caleb that I knew I would cherish for eternity.

I hadn't any idea how much time had passed, but when I raised, we were parked in a car rental area of the airport. We'd arrived, and with good timing. Caleb still appeared elated.

The driver's door slammed with excessive force.

Caleb pulled my chin, so I looked at him. "I love you so much already, little Jules."

This did feel a bit like a fairy tale when it came to Caleb. The non-abusive kidnapper, who'd already grown attached to his prize. He could just as easily be my knight in shining armor who whisked me away from a lair of wealthy evil men.

The brother who yanked open the back and slammed the luggage down would be a different story. John wanted a slave. And that could only be romanticized to a certain amount. No, he was definitely not the sort of person I wanted taking over my life.

That clunky noise gave me a bit of hope, though. My plane ticket back home was in a satchel in my suitcase. My current itinerary departed around 5:40 AM. It may have currently only been about one in the morning.

If I could get that ticket and rush away at the time of my original flight, I would escape. They wouldn't even bother coming for me for the fear of being arrested and having their wealthy friends discovered. Everything would work out perfectly. More than perfectly. We would all have a fun memory from this endeavor. At least Caleb and I would.

Daring Escape

I had little experience in airports, but I could assume that seeing a gas-lamp brothel woman with a corset and ruffles would be odd. Leather cuffs should draw attention, right?

Wrong. Nobody cared, aside from a few lechers who wanted to spy if I was wearing any panties under the short dress.

I wasn't even a security risk the TSA would pay special mind to. Then again, the line we went through had a man deep in conversation with John. Was it a friendly conversation? Maybe the agent was accepting a bribe so they could shuffle me forward without complication.

I couldn't trust anyone here to help me. Cops might only tase and silence me.

I clung to Caleb, twining fingers with his to ensure him he could trust me. So far, I'd been successful. My bindings weren't latched together behind my back, which was most important.

I'd also managed a quick scan of my bag as they found my identification. My ticket to return home originally waited in the satchel near the top, and it had been easy to pluck and slide beneath my corset as the brothers argued with each other while their backs were to me.

They seemed to have interpersonal issues that weren't conducive to co-owning a woman. My leaving would be in their best interest. And, given their preoccupation with whatever they mumbled about, my repeated trips to the bathroom and food machines eventually had Caleb giving me a modest distance for a few minutes at a time.

About five minutes after the call to board my home flight, I got up just like I was about to toss some trash and go to the bathroom again.

"I'll win." Caleb's words in his low discussion with his brother made the moment even more memorable. He would win whatever they discussed, but I would sneak away with my victory in sight.

John's watchful green eyes didn't have the usual bite when I cast him a last glance, more of a satisfaction at his perceived success.

But he hadn't won. I won. I was free of them. And I gloated on that breezy escape during the flight home.

Ridiculous as it may have been, I also found myself wishing I'd had more time with them. More of the fun of struggling against all odds to get home. In any book, the heroine would have had every escape route blocked. People would have been injured, and I would have been thoroughly and unequivocally punished after my failed attempt at freedom.

Now I could only rest in my seat and fantasize about how the moment of certain failure would have played out. The way Caleb would bend me over and punish me with his raging manhood. Then John might do the same, but he'd hold that last stare of satisfaction as he claimed me again and again. At least, in my fantasy, he had a right to the triumphant expression he'd maintained when I parted ways with them.

The flight was an adrenaline rush of doubt in my own ability to survive and escape. I wasn't idle. I had a goal I would achieve. But true success became cemented when I landed on solid ground, and the brothers weren't around to stop me. There were no devious smiles that taunted me, only me proving my dedication to my happiness.

In all my life, success wasn't really something I did. Success required reason for initiative. I never had that before. Aside from my work as a florist, I'd had no goals. Outside of small-town drama, which I rarely became involved in, nothing exciting ever happened. But I rose to this new challenge with an absolutely unstoppable force to survive.

My toes bounced when it was my turn to rise and make my way down the aisle and out of the plane. If only Caleb could have seen me, he would have been proud. But that would've come with its own problems, so I didn't want the opportunity to gloat.

Too much energy jittered within me as I slowly shuffled behind other fliers to deboard the plane. What I hadn't expected as I stepped out of the aircraft was my purple luggage waiting at the beginning of the long hall.

I brought nothing with me aside from what I wore. That luggage shouldn't have been there. Any elation from moments earlier crashed down, shredding my sense of achievement. From a string connected to the handle, a white envelope happily dangled. Its tilt looked more like a malicious smirk that my luggage bore.

John's last triumphant expression burned into my mind as I slid the lavender card from the crisp envelope. The messy letters inked inside looked like long scratches.

Slave—You will be punished.

Then another word was on the opposite side. This writing would have been beautiful if not for the single word.

severely.

The second had to be Caleb's response. He'd never called me a slave; his brother declared that was my status.

I searched the walkway and the people who briskly moved past. The brothers hadn't been passengers aboard the plane. I would have seen them. The most unnerving part about this fresh development was my loss of Caleb as an ally. He wasn't on my side anymore. I'd decimated any future trust and protection he would have provided.

Severely. The beautifully written cursive flashed behind my eyelids again. I'd gone about this all wrong.

John's expression during that last conversation between them spoke of who truly won. He did. And I'd fallen into his well-laid plan, whatever that plan may prove to be.

Blossoming Attraction

Real World

The brothers didn't pounce on me while I cautiously navigated the airport. They didn't even show up outside in the parking lot. Everything went on perfectly normally in the mundane world I returned to.

I'd had the passionate high of playing the heroine of a mildly steamy dark romance, but I couldn't go home and revel in the afterglow. I hadn't won. Any memory was now polluted with the fear of what the future held.

After a few days of biting my nails and absently checking for orders, my paranoia led me to call up Roy, the guy I occasionally dated.

He'd been my classmate all the way from kindergarten to senior graduation, but his scruff and belly could pass him as a man in his thirties. Some people we grew up with found him attractive, but he lacked the chiseled jaw and cunning stare of an antihero. He probably didn't even know a suit was an article of clothing. Not that the lack of exposure mattered.

"About damn time we went out again," he said with a sharp twang. He finished his beer and slapped the mug onto the table before examining a warped pool stick for the round we would play.

How had I ever–*ever*–had sex with him? Even at his best, I couldn't free my mind to experience someone dark and brooding. I couldn't close my eyes and let an intruder have his way. Sex was simply Roy on top of me or, when he occasionally felt adventurous, behind me for about one minute. I couldn't even imagine him as a sultan who'd captured me for his harem that I needed to escape. Nothing made him superb.

I could have had a hot Toyota driver. Two hot ones. Not billionaire mafia sorts, but still the sort of sexy that could have panties drenched from afar. Why had I even wanted to come home? Right now, I should be experiencing adoration from Caleb or being mercilessly ravished by John.

"You ain't eating," Roy said, though his concern was for the food left untouched on my plate.

"Have it," I muttered, pushing the dish in his direction.

If only a mask could make Roy more appealing to me, I'd find one with a wolf design. I could let this scene take hold and imagine the nachos were a specialty from a far-away, paranormal celebration. The crackly music might then sound divine. But he could never be a tenth as magnificent as one of the brothers who'd almost captured me.

I couldn't stop my mind from wandering to them coming for me. Reimagining the way John threatened to ravish me. How good it felt when he ripped the neckline of my top and freed my breast from the tight corset.

Roy clogged my vision as he attempted a sashay. "Been a real while since you looked at me with that kind of lust." He smoothed his dark bangs to the side.

Instead of John's commanding hold latching around my waist, Roy pawed at me like a needy puppy. "Maybe me and you could make ourselves pretty busy making some babies after this."

God no!

This was why I preferred being at home with a good book and no one else to bother me. And it was precisely why I fantasized about all sorts of deviant sex that wouldn't have such horrendous consequences as a baby.

My phone rang with a deep and ominous ringtone I'd never set. It wasn't my imagination, either. Classical cello.

Green eyes toyed with my mind, darkly predatory behind a wolf's mask. The brothers might finally make a move. One I'd been imagining in every waking moment since returning to the depressing place I once imagined with a twist of dark pleasure.

Roy dug the phone out of my back pocket, flashing his best, albeit cheesy, smile. He may have thought touching me in such a way was flirting, but it fell a good bit short, and made me want to run somewhere to get away from him so I could let my imagination play out.

The most likely caller, on the other hand, had me wanting to flee for other reasons. Maybe I did want to play a game of cat and mouse, but not with Roy around. Not while I looked like an exhausted wreck. And *not* in real life.

I snatched my phone from him and checked for the caller.

Unknown Number.

Answering the call seemed better than acknowledging Roy's behavior. Knowing it might be one of the brothers brought a bit of heat to my tummy. "Hello."

"I don't like how you've been letting him so close to you." The angry voice could have been John or Caleb. Whichever brother spoke to me must have been somewhere other than this local dive, given I could see everyone here.

"You talking to another man all sexy-like?" Roy muttered, reaching and grabbing my phone from my hand.

I hadn't answered in a sexy tone, had I? What business of his would the conversation be, anyway?

"Give it—" I grabbed for the phone, but the tipsy jerk spun on his toes with it to his ear.

"Who's calling my girlfriend?" Roy spoke loud to ensure the handful of people in the bar heard him.

"I'm not your girlfriend!" I never had been. I wouldn't even be able to unbutton my jeans in front of Roy after having experienced Caleb and John.

Roy turned my way. "Julie don't have a fiancée." His tone and strengthening of his accent seemed mad, even emotionally hurt when he looked at me. "You been cheating on me with some city fellow?"

I shook my head, startled by the level of insanity Roy suffered if he really believed we were a couple. I also felt bad for him, given the way his voice cracked. I'd been clear that relationships weren't my thing.

"Guy here says you've been cheating." He slammed his pool cue upright against the table with a loud thwack.

"I'm *not* your girlfriend." I felt guilty for however bad he must have felt. I hadn't even known it mattered so much to him. I twisted my shoulder backward when Roy reached for me with his free hand while he held my phone to his ear.

I could get my phone at another time instead of dealing with this confrontation. While he grumbled something, I went to the bar and waved for the tab. I spoke to the bartender, "Make sure someone drives him home, please."

The owner, Mike, cocked a brow and huffed as he took a few twenties I handed him. "About time, Julie." He counted out change and leaned forward to hand it to me. "Maybe me and you..."

God. Another fucking guy wanting a date. Mike was only a little older than me at mid twenties. He was well established with his own business, extremely attractive, and also engaged.

"Keep it," I muttered, leaving the change as a tip. I rushed toward the crooked wooden door, yanking it open for the crisp evening night.

I got the fresh air in a sharp gasp at the sight of Caleb standing beside the open passenger door of a silver Subaru Forester that had stopped sideways at the entry of the bar. The streetlight illuminated the obvious tick to his jaw as he lowered the phone from his ear. He was still sexy as sin, especially since his topknot had been freed to let dark hair fall to the shoulder of his black peacoat.

Roy's grumbling came close behind, but not before Caleb shoved his phone in his pocket.

"Get in, Jules," the younger brother said.

I could run from Caleb. Continue to pretend there was hope of escape from this man who'd made certain to claim me.

"My girl ain't going." Roy charged toward me as I hastily fled toward Caleb. To the refuge of the Subaru and escape from the dreary reality of what I'd returned to.

Home

Aside from the phone conversation and the order to get in the Subaru, Caleb hadn't spoken to me. Silent seconds became minutes that were more awkward as he drove the lonely highway. He'd kept this unexpected reunion unnerving.

"Where's John?" I asked nervously after about five minutes.

"Bringing the dungeon," Caleb replied, terse.

"Oh." I watched the passing darkness as I thought back to the promise of a mobile dungeon. They actually had one of those and intended to keep me captive in it? And Caleb just told the one person who would miss me that I was engaged. I would simply vanish without suspicion.

"It's a long trip." He slowed at the gravel driveway I lived down.

"You found me fast." I fidgeted in my seat.

"I took the flight scheduled an hour after yours."

Not that we could see each other very well in the darkness, but I knew he looked my direction when his voice increased slightly. He'd been stalking me these days. No wonder he knew perfectly where I lived.

"Oh." It was a dumb word to repeat.

"John hired drivers to help speed up his travel while he designs and installs a proper dungeon."

How large would the mentioned dungeon be in an RV? I'd concluded that the brothers weren't billionaire antiheroes. They were probably middle-class American guys willing to pay to own someone. And there weren't any happily ever after sort of books with that kind of kidnapper. Those were the horror news articles—especially if the guys were hot and seductive.

But even the thought of being spread eagle tied on my back in an RV bed awaiting these two brothers had me crossing my legs as the throb set in. Maybe even being bent over to accept a painful belting for my attempt to run away from the real-world insanity of it all.

The vehicle stopped in front of the brick home I'd shared with my grandmother before she died and willed her home and the floral business to me. Not that there'd been anyone else in line for the inheritance. Just me.

I couldn't help mentioning the note to Caleb that he and John left on my luggage. "You mentioned punishment."

He got out, came around, and opened my door. As I stepped out, he said, "I only mentioned that it would be severe." He turned and led me to my home.

He still refused to be the sweet beta I betrayed at the airport.

Every pebble beneath my tennis shoes crackled as I walked past him and dug my keys from my clutch. The trembling of my hand made the key nearly impossible to line up to the lock.

Something would happen to me, with severity being a certainty. If only it would happen already.

I couldn't handle the secret craving I had for him to glide a hand up my back. For his fist to tangle into my hair as it did while I sucked his cock in the back seat of the measly Toyota. To be severely tossed onto my couch after I unlocked the door and stepped inside—forced to utter submission.

I didn't immediately turn on the light inside my home once I took the tumultuous steps in. He didn't need to see this recent mess that had accrued after my return to mope in the misery of my boring, passionless life.

Caleb flipped the light-switch and awaken the mess.

"I haven't been well," I muttered. It was a poor defense of the clutter.

Part of why I once loved to keep a cleaner home had been the fantasy of punishment by an ever-watchful Master who lorded over me without mercy. But after experiencing Caleb and John, that fantasy didn't feel as satisfying. I became depressed, and even more books pulled me from livelihood.

"John will train you to keep house." He still didn't soften toward me. After removing his wool coat, he tossed it on a chair piled with order slips for floral services. Several of the forms crashed onto the floor.

I dared not remove my thin jacket for fear he would see I'd taken off the purple-lined leather cuffs. That was a captive's no-no that deserved severe penalties.

As he stepped further into my home, I had to rush to the coffee table to grab the four old romance novels I'd reread.

"They're nothing," I muttered. I felt the shame of the addiction that no one understood. I should've already popped out two kids by now. Most of my high school classmates had their second baby before they could legally enter a bar. Then there was me, willingly unattached.

Caleb plucked one book from my hold. "They look like books to me."

He already knew I wasn't into the sort of gentle hero like in old romance novels with bent and frayed covers. We'd discussed books of a darker tone, and, for a while, I got to live the life I loved to be immersed in. I felt guilty for having used his kindness as a means for escape. I'd truly loved his company.

Caleb and John weren't fantasies, though, and I'd needed to get away from them. Sure, the current painless suspense was addictive, but being theirs meant the uncertainty of things to come and the absolute loss of control over my life. At least the billionaire antiheroes in the stories made every moment of servitude absolutely delicious.

Even if he didn't fit the men I gobbled up stories about, I couldn't deny how Caleb's presence still drew me to him. The encounter still seemed strange, like he still wasn't a captor, only a reluctant minion.

"Did John force you to wait outside and stalk me?" I asked.

Nonchalantly, he tossed the book onto the coffee table, knocking over an empty cup. "I can't stalk something I already own."

"It's not like you act like it," I muttered under my breath, too low to be heard. I clutched the books to my chest, looking up at Caleb's perfect face as he took the swift step to tower directly in front of me.

He scowled. "I heard that." The way he assessed me with lustful intent turned my will to fight him into mush.

"What does severely mean?" I breathed.

He licked his lower lip at the same time I bit mine. Now, I wanted the severely that might have me thrown down by this man who claimed to own me.

"Severely," he said, taking the books I clutched at my chest and tossing them toward the coffee table with a clatter. "Means the dungeon requires upgrades for punishing a very, *very* bad slave who doesn't feel owned yet." His fist finally raised to my nape, firmly tugging.

"Punishing?" I breathed, my need building despite all reason.

This wouldn't be like the novels. But I'd already fantasized about the brothers too much. This moment might lead me to my doom.

I should have called the cops on them the moment my plane had landed, but I'd wanted to imagine I could experience the danger again. To be consumed by a longing for how they would come and take me. That couldn't have happened if cops were contacting me, or if the brothers had been arrested. Those were all boring outcomes that caused closure to a fantasy I never wanted to end.

"You ran away under my watch. Just as John wagered you would." Caleb brought back the memory of him and John at the airport mentioning winning.

"And what did he win?" I asked.

"He gets to unleash his sadist side." Caleb didn't bother asking permission before reaching his free hand to my jacket zipper and guiding it all the way down.

He would see that I no longer wore the cuffs. He might react as any angry Master would. He might...punish me.

I panted, slightly hissing as the hold to the back of my head forced me to look upward. Dark and brooding—God, did he turn magnificently dark and brooding.

Did this beta have a sadist side? Just the thought sent my being into another universe. It was an idiotic desire to want this to play out like the smut I loved. His closeness felt drugging, though. Like it awoke my addiction to the idea of being dominated by someone so sexy as he was.

Caleb freed his hand from my hair, preferring to guide the sleeves down my arms and let the jacket fall.

My fists clenched as his fingertips tickled along my exposed wrists. *Damn it. Damn it. Damn it.* He knew I no longer wore the cuffs.

"Are you a sadist too?" I whispered.

Would I enjoy it if he was? Most definitely not once the pain came.

Some of his hair tickled my nose, feeling like a long-wanted breeze against my face as he closed in. I loved his towering height. His strength. And his ability to rule over me if he desired.

"There are other ways to break bad behaviors," he purred close enough to kiss me. Maybe my irresistible beta did return.

I blinked several times as my eyes focused on his. "Such as?" I asked, heart skipping at the possibilities. I wanted him to tangle his fist in my hair again.

"Binding you to a bed." He kissed me, but it was only a teasing peck. "But you took off the cuffs I picked out just for you." His palms glid up my arms, smooth and caring.

"They're at my shop," I breathed, chilled from the air against my skin. But an inferno took hold of me from within.

Although I'd needed wire cutters to break the small padlocks, I couldn't bring myself to damage the cuffs. I'd loved seeing them and continued fantasizing about the day he would capture and bind me with them.

He didn't need to know that, though.

He placed another peck. "That's not very far away, now is it?"

Just a short walk up the gravel path. Two minutes straight there. Five if I go slow to admire the moonlight reflecting on the road-side pond, but the early-spring evening temperature was too cold for that sort of stroll.

It certainly wouldn't be a romantic stroll. Maybe one where I attempted to escape, and he had to throw me down to put me in my place. Or possibly I would free myself and lock him out of the floral shop. There wasn't a phone to call someone for help, though. Nor would the sole town cop be sober.

"It's not far at all," I replied, probably after too long of a wait.

Flowers

Caleb went over to the chair his coat rested on. He dug something out of the side pocket before flashing a deceptively innocent grin in my direction. "I guess you and I are about to go on our first moonlit walk together."

The smile genuinely worried me. Like, maybe he was one of those hot guys from the werewolf novels ready to lead me out into the full moon before shifting forms. I didn't even know if he was beta anymore. Could that even change?

Black shone from his hand as he pulled something from his pocket. A thick leather that matched the black and purple of the cuffs he'd used on me. Escape might not be so easy.

A collar.

If this was a walk, that was a collar. And I definitely caught sight of the thick band he fisted. But there was gravel outside. My knees would get hurt.

He did use the word *walk*.

Cooperation would surely keep my knees unharmed. Besides, John was the sadist. This had to be the sweet beta that would make the two of them tolerable. No romance novel ever had a bad and worse captor—at least none that kept my interest.

But just in case I was wrong about him being the good brother, I did the only smart thing and pulled my brown hair to the back of my head and lifted it in an act of submission.

"That's my good girl, Jules." Caleb prowled the few steps my way, raising the leather that had soft purple suede to cushion the skin. The tinkling of metal as he wrapped my neck and tightened the captivity device didn't raise any alarm. The clicks were what informed me it had locks sealed to ensure I couldn't easily remove it.

I turned, but he stopped me with a single pull to the ring at the front of the collar.

"I need my jacket," I said.

"It's a short walk." He slid his hand along about five feet of length of the thin black leather leash he attached to the collar. "Let's go."

He let me gather my keys, but nothing more. And he wrapped himself up in his coat again.

As his captive, or slave, or whatever I was to him, I wouldn't deserve the same simple comforts as he had. And the moment he opened the door, I realized just how much of a luxury an extra layer would have been. It must have been in the low fifties outside.

There was something sexy about this, though. A bit at his mercy, cold and on a mission, and a possibility for escape, so this could play out romantically in my mind. After all, they weren't the sort of bad boy billionaires I fantasized about. Therefore, no matter the excitement, the real-world consequences weren't worth actually going with them to be their RV sex slave.

"What are you planning to do once you have me inescapably re-strained?" I hesitantly asked, holding back a chatter of my teeth.

He let the leash curl over my shoulder and took my hand in his. This was just a cold, romantic stroll. This fine-as-sin man being all cuddly on a quest for more items to immobilize and bind me. Nothing I hadn't already imagined at least a dozen times.

"I never said anything about inescapable restraints," he replied.

"So they're just for show?" I asked, walking at his side to accept his warmth.

As it was, the leash to keep me contained wasn't in use. He could always grab and yank it if needed, which was precisely why I didn't bother plotting to push him into the cold, placid pond that perfectly reflected the moon.

I thought about it, though. Oh, did I think about the way he would almost grab the dangling leather. The feel of his strong hands as they barely missed capturing me. The soaked hair hanging down when he finally caught up to me.

The excitement built too much. I couldn't get far, I knew that. But the thought of him peeling away a drenched shirt to reveal his muscles as he loomed over me had me leaning toward testing the situation. There would be no escaping the sort of punishment to come from such a misdeed, though.

"I know how to handle a little fox like you," he replied, dragging me from the fantasy of being overpowered.

It felt like I'd just plotted our next interaction in those few seconds. I still had time to think about whether I should push him in and run to my shop, only to fail to get the key in the door in time and escape him.

My muscles already shook, though. Holding the key already felt like it might not come easily.

The time for acting out such a misdeed came and went, and soon enough, we reached the massive front window of my unlit floral shop. At that point, holding my keys steady proved to be impossible.

Caleb had to take them from me and unlock the rickety door. All the while, I watched the clouds of steamy breaths escape me in slow motion.

The way he held the door open with a foot and how he looped an arm around me to lead me into the fragrant warmth felt so gentlemanly. It felt so...charming. But still in a fun, and mildly dangerous, bad boy sort of way.

Cuffed

The thing about this time of year, as spring awoke, was the abundance of flowers that I kept on demand and all the events that constantly occurred. And, given I'd been depressed and in my own world lately, this little haven of freshness seemed neglected. The small shop may have been filled with varying flowers for upcoming events, but I hadn't given many of them fabulous designs yet. It looked only slightly nicer than an unkempt grocery store floral department.

But the fragrance felt like every romance I'd ever read, giving me a high of euphoria. Who couldn't love the smell of roses and carnations? Or the way a vibrant moon's light pouring into the display window played on the blooms of orchids.

Even music came to life in my head. Wedding music to start, but slowly creeping into the strings from the night I met the antihero and beta. A sort of menacing sound, and as Caleb and I wove to the cooled display with roses, even the feel of that night overcame me with the abundance of smell.

I could fantasize about being laid out on the dais. A sacrifice, bound and awaiting her fate at the hands of a man with bronzed skin and a tropical sort of sexiness. A man who could do any number of things to my helpless but hungering being that awaited him.

The heat building within me demanded I find those cuffs quickly. By God, in all reality, I needed to be dominated. Ideally, before John arrived. I could entice Caleb to have his way with me. Do things I could have only ever fantasized about, then simply get away. Truly get away. That way, this wouldn't end with me miserable and suffering as their slave.

Caleb would make this fun and still leave things open to my imagination. And the more that enrapturous music played in my mind and the smell of our first meeting took hold, I lost myself to the desire to be ravished by this perfect man.

We continued to the back area that was also in need of organization. This would end perfectly. As soon as I got to experience his control, my life would bounce back to what it had been. This la-la land of imagination could end, and I could be productive again.

Still where I left them on a short table, the cuffs practically called to me. Black leather and purple suede to cushion it. He'd chosen my favorite color. Maybe he'd been stalking me for years and I simply never knew.

"How did you know purple was my favorite color?" I breathed the words, my heart fluttering at the thought.

He'd had his hand to my back and stood behind me, but his answer included his erection pressed to my back. After his arms curled around me, his airy words were spoken against the hair over my ear. "It was on your social media page. The color you always wore. The flowers you most often chose."

That really had me in overdrive. They did their research after seeing me online. I wasn't some cheap, last-minute purchase—if that story of purchasing me even held any truth.

"I had to special order them at the same time John bought all the black roses from multiple states to see you beam as you so caringly designed an event in the theme of your favorite book." He directed both my wrists in front of my stomach, holding them there with one hand while walking me forward so he could collect the cuffs.

In a twisted, billionaire fiction sort of way, his story seemed quite romantic. But why a small-town nobody? Why not someone beautiful and perfect and raised to be proper?

"What made me so special?" I asked, not fighting as he placed the restraint on my wrist, carefully clicking the lock.

"For me, it was that *O* shape of your lips when you're delighted," he said. "The girl next door look." He buckled and locked the other cuff to my left wrist. "But you stopped soon after your granma died."

That made me feel ashamed of myself. I'd let down the people who enjoyed the novel themed floral designs. "Oh."

"It was John who was jacking off to one of your videos when you had a pouty expression." Caleb reminded me of the sadist who planned to co-own me. Now the beta's lips were on my neck, warming me. "We both wanted you, and now we have you."

And if they did that much research, they really did have me. There wasn't a place I could go that Caleb probably hadn't already followed me to.

Foolishly, that excited me more. His erection scraped against my lower back, teasingly cruel.

But they rode in middle class cars. They weren't billionaire anti-heroes. This could all be a lie. They wouldn't have been able to afford the decorations or come up with such a lavish event as the masquerade I'd decorated.

"Why didn't you pick me up in a BMW? That's what the uber wealthy drive." I immediately felt stupid. I should have said Lamborghini or something. Or demand to know where his chauffeur had been.

"Only egotistical fucks with small dicks feel the need to lure women with a high-priced car," he replied.

Caleb had no small dick. He should have been in a Kia since he wasn't making up for insecurities in the manhood department.

The hold to my bound hands shifted to an embrace, with one of his hands groping at my left breast. "I wanted to be the one to have you first."

"I won't stop you," I replied, feeling a bit fearful of this ravenous desire between my legs going nowhere. I wanted—no, I needed—for this man to claim my body in ways I only got to read about in secrecy.

"John wants to know the first baby is his." The pads of his fingers stroked my breast.

Maybe this wouldn't play out so fun after all. Adding a newborn to the mental images and music in my head ruined the excitement for me. Again, imagination would always win over reality.

Now that the fun of the predicament fell flat, I came back to the reality of how stupid it would be to be taken by this man. Domination and dungeons were slowly intriguing me, but babies had the opposite effect.

But the cuffs were already connected, so my wrists would remain connected in front of me. He'd been smart enough to have brought small padlocks with him, so they were secured well.

It seemed my life was doomed to be a misery. All I could do was fantasize about a perfect life of dark romance or be content with someone like Roy and pop out children. No, children weren't my thing. Not even if it was a breeder captor's baby kink.

"Go clear the counter and lay on it for me, baby girl." Caleb released me to return to the front section of the shop.

Even with bound hands, I made quick work of moving supplies and fresh flowers from the waist-height surface. It wasn't a length for my whole body, so when I lay onto it, my head almost bumped the wall and my mid thighs and beyond were unsupported.

Caleb pulled me so my hips were at the edge, unfastening and then removing my jeans.

Heat consumed me. Like an inferno bursting from my traitorous body. Like all those stories with women who irrationally wanted to be fucked by their captors and where the lines of consent blurred. That line had been blurring since the first words John spoke to me.

I couldn't act like a *yo-yo* and be indecisive, though. In no way would that be graceful or fulfilling. But this man already said he wouldn't fuck me.

I attempted a fearful voice. "What are you going to do to me?"

He smirked, peeling my panties down my legs, so they fell to the floor. "First, I'm going to punish you." He pushed my legs wide apart. "Then I'm going to punish you some more." His eyes may have remained on mine, but he knew exactly how to locate the bundle of nerves that was so eager to be found.

"Punish?" I waited, worried, but not as concerned for my wellbeing as someone in my position should be. It was his charm that kept hypnotizing me. Any girl into non-con fantasies could fall under the spell of a man like him. And, not to mention, I liked the idea of being shaved smooth with a core worthy of admiration.

"I'm going to get you so close. You're going to be pleading for me to let you have an orgasm." He finally looked down to the folds, spreading them to have a look. "You've been too bad to be rewarded with release, though, haven't you?"

Was this a threat? A plan to almost force me to have an orgasm. Dragging it out. But I supposed those were better than forcing orgasms until my body just couldn't take it anymore.

"I..." how to answer. I didn't want him to decide the punishment should go the other way around. Repeated orgasms would be horrible, not to mention shameful to be seen. That also seemed like something someone sadistic, like John, might do if the two brothers considered orgasms to be a means of punishment.

"My bed?" I asked, hoping to be given a bit more freedom and possibly ask to have my wrists unbound.

"John's the sentimental sort. Flowers and romantic music might make him a little less eager to punish you," he said as he pushed my shirt up, catching my bra as well until they went as high as they could go on my sternum, exposing my breasts. "Raise your arms."

As I moved my bound hands to the top of my head, I wondered why the flowers in the shop would protect me? Maybe the blooms and music were the only thing that had stopped the villainous older brother from getting carried away the night we met.

Caleb reached up to my breasts, grabbing the left one, seeming to be turned on by the sight. "God, I want to fuck you so badly." His other fingers slowly worked over my nub. "That's right, Jules, fight it. I want this to last a while."

Sure, he may have wanted that, but how could I not think of all the times I wanted a man to do this to me? Or the way they'd touched me at the masquerade?

Fuck! It had been less than a minute and I already couldn't take my mind off of how good that secret desire of mine was as it came true.

Caleb couldn't be that bad of a guy if he wanted to ensure John arrived in a situation that would prevent his sadist side from taking over. The younger brother continued to toy with me, switching his hold from one breast to the other, tormenting me as his touch slowed.

Fuck him for making this feel so good. Damn him for refusing to ravish me in this shop where I'd always wanted someone handsome to force their way in at closing time and have flowers strewn about as they pulled me toward the back.

"Oh Jules, that look on your face is turning me on too much."

I knew my eyes were rolling upward and my bottom lip was between my teeth, but those alone couldn't have been that sexy. Even still, I couldn't help but imagine how much this beta wanted me, the perfect woman for him to own.

"Please," I moaned. Let him succumb to his lust. Even if it enraged his older brother, and I suffered punishment before my escape, I would always cherish the memory. I would happily become a satisfied old spinster, knowing I'd experienced such bliss.

Found

"I want you to suck my cock, then I'll decide if you've earned an orgasm." His hands went to my waist, spinning me on the counter, so my knees had to bend all the way to my chest and my head tilted at an angle for his manhood to enter. "I'm going to train this throat of yours, baby." Within seconds, his cock sprang free and pushed against my lips.

I didn't fight its entry; I wanted for him to claim it again. I spread my legs wide, reaching my bound wrists down to touch myself.

"Nuh uh, baby girl." He plunged deep and grabbed the fasten between the cuffs, pulling them up to my stomach. The halt as he pressed at the back of my throat hindered my breath and had me close to gagging, but he seemed to know how to control when I could breathe and stop the gag.

Why couldn't he continue to tease me with an orgasm, possibly getting carried away with his pleasure and take me so far I couldn't hold back? He could punish me all he wanted to afterward. Only a few seconds after his firm hands found my breasts, I heard the jangle of the entry door.

Though muffled, I heard a familiar voice. Roy's voice. And it drew closer as he spoke. "What in the fuck are you doing with my girl?"

Damn it, Roy. He ruined every joy in my imaginary world, now he interfered with this perfect moment. I tried to twist free, but Caleb's motions continued.

"I'm letting my fiancée suck my dick." He spoke of me as his yet again. A permanency to this relationship between us. No one married their property, though. This was setting up for when I disappeared.

"I'll shoot ya," Roy warned.

At that threat, I swung my arms back, surprising Caleb enough his cock went far enough out that I could turn, panting as I got a huge gulp of air. "What is wrong with you, Roy?" I spun to stand, defending my captor with my minimally covered body that Roy took in the sight of.

He didn't have a gun in his hands, nor did I see one on his belt. "You *have* been cheating!"

"Care to watch?" At those haughty words, Caleb pulled me to the side, facing Roy as I was bent over the counter. The massive manhood I'd hardly handled in my mouth plunged into me.

Horror replaced Roy's anger as he stared at us like a deer in a spotlight. He didn't even move as Caleb's hips reared back and slammed into me again.

Then the explosion hit. Copious amounts of seed shot straight to my cervix. That wasn't what I'd wanted at all. It set precedent to cum in me in the future. No babies, not from Caleb or John.

Roy knew I never had unprotected sex. Maybe that was the reason he still stood motionless. He was a fairly nice country guy, hoping to settle down with someone and have a family, and I wasn't that kind of girl.

"Clearly, she prefers me." Caleb kept his collected attitude, as though he loved being watched.

Roy may have threatened violence, but he'd switched to a look of despair when he pointed at me. "You ain't going to be happy with no one."

And there went the reality of my life. I wouldn't be happy with anyone. My vibrator and my books and every man I dreamed about were all I needed. And, of course, the memory of how Caleb had just dominated me.

"She doesn't want you," Caleb said, unmoving behind me.

My eyes squeezed shut from the sting of my cruelty to him. I hadn't meant to hurt him. "I'm sorry, Roy."

Clearly, he considered the occasional dates and sex as my faithfulness to him. I wasn't certain why or how, and I preferred not thinking about it.

"You ain't nothing to me. Don't even come back to Mama's house or one of her parties ever again, you sinning harlot."

It wasn't like I did those things, anyway. But his mother referred so much business to me that losing her meant I lost a large amount of income. Not to mention, everyone up to ten towns over would hear about me being caught *cheating* and *sinning*.

"Nobody talks to my Jules that way!" Caleb snapped, far harsher than I would have imagined him capable of. "Get the fuck out, douchebag!"

I turned at my waist to stop the escalation, but Roy already burst the door open and stormed out. It was all I could do to balance forward and force my bound hands to jerk my top and bra down.

"I'm not done with those yet, baby girl." Caleb reached around me to dig beneath my shirt and fondle my breasts some more.

His cock hadn't freed me yet. It had hardly shrunk. He may have been trying to rile me more by massaging my breasts, but I'd already lost interest in what was happening.

"Now then, where were we before that self-absorbed prick interrupted us?" He thrust further into me, his cock still ready for more. It became impossible to not want him when his fingers found that spot that craved his touch yet again.

The way I leaned forward welcomed him into me more. I winced at the massive size, and he responded with slower movements.

Right now, as he stroked and pumped into me, I was happier than I'd ever been in the clutches of a man. It felt more real. Sure, I still needed to know I had absolutely no control, but that was what fantasies were about. He seemed too close to precisely what I wanted in a man.

"Just because I let you cum this once doesn't mean you aren't in trouble for running away." His fingertips set me ablaze, awakening me to the sort of bliss I could never provide myself with. It felt so real.

It *was* real.

"Strangle my cock, Jules." He pistoned faster, still careful not to go too deep or use full force. He'd gotten me back to that holy place he teased me with before Roy interrupted us. That hovering at the edge of bliss. But now, he let me have that moment of release.

As the orgasm consumed me, he thrust deep, but I could only feel the pulses of delight. The clenching of my gratification drank whatever remaining seed he had left to give me. We both collapsed forward onto the counter, with him finally breaking the connection inside me.

John's Return

C aleb decided it was best to disconnect the cuffs on my wrists so I could use a wet cloth to cleanse all evidence of our coupling. "John is a bit..." His lips quirked to the side in a way that suggested he was searching for polite words. "OCD. We should probably make the place look extra presentable to win over his softer side."

And I quickly went to work organizing the flowers and perfecting their angles and where they were located. Caleb hadn't specifically mentioned that his brother might come at any minute, but the reason he'd brought me out to the flower shop had been for his brother's arrival. I wouldn't have thought Caleb could be any more thoughtful, but he even found classical music to play on low.

Wedding music, but I supposed I didn't have many other selections to choose from, given it was an old CD he'd found. Roy still had my phone, which would have had the selection of music I preferred. For over an hour, we tidied up the shop. Then we saw high-set lights shine in as a vehicle pulled into my driveway.

With Caleb, I felt like I had more control over the outcome, but not John. I remembered he wasn't the sort to be played with. Even the comments about his car infuriated him. He would react like a monster if he knew what I'd done with Caleb. We both knew better than to say a word.

The minutes ticked by slowly after the large vehicle stopped for a while. I waited with my wrists bound behind my back while seated on the counter. I needed to look punished by Caleb, who wasn't actually the sort capable of punishing me to the extent I loved to imagine happening. But I knew to be thankful for that.

The lights turned off from where it remained parked closer to my house than to the shop. Was the guy going to snoop through my home?

"How much did you pay for me?" I asked Caleb. Hopefully, he would be honest.

He smirked from where he leaned against the wall with his arms crossed. "There are a lot of fees that go into ensuring no problems occur when selecting someone. And you weren't exactly someone easily available."

Whatever did that mean? Fees. Like I hadn't already been kidnapped? I pondered on these words. But all I found to ask was "why?"

But he'd already told me the reason. They saw me. They wanted me. And his brother even jacked off to an image or brief video of me with flowers. Even at the sight of me fully clothed and average, John already knew he wanted me.

"You're hot stuff." As soon as Caleb said those words, the lightweight door burst open as though it had been kicked. And it must have been.

Roy soon toppled into the shop, knocking vases and flowers down. So much for the secret I shared with Caleb.

Behind him was the fiercest expression I'd ever seen. Passionate and one thousand percent sexy. Sexy, at least, if John wasn't a real flesh-and-blood man whose fury seemed set on me.

"Turn that fucking music off!" John spat.

One effort to calm him failed.

As Caleb rushed to the CD player, John said, "Found this person peeping outside the house? And he told me you've been having a bit of fun with a few men while you came home to pack."

"It's true. I ain't peeping or lying." Roy pointed up to Caleb. "She's been cheating with that man and claiming he's her fiancée." Roy scurried to his feet, almost slipping on water from a toppled vase. "Just swindling all of us for all she can get."

Caleb huffed, and I wasn't certain if it was disgust or humor with Roy's accusation.

The reality was that Roy never paid for a damned thing. I took absolutely nothing from him. It was shocking to hear such delusions. Pity for him rapidly became harder and harder to reason. I would have offered a retort if John's glower didn't harbor daggers. And it was aimed at me.

This was when dark romance lost all of its charm. This became too real. I knew better than to do anything at all. If only I could melt into nothingness to escape this obnoxiously handsome man.

"Make sure this kind gentleman makes it home safely. And give him back the few hundred dollars *my fiancée* swindled from him." John prowled my way, not bothering to look at a single bloom I'd so delicately placed. I forgot about the collar on my neck until his attention focused on it. He probably wouldn't be the playful sort to let the leash hang free, as Caleb had.

Caleb quickly strode outside, with Roy skulking behind. My sweet beta left me alone with an infuriated sadist.

I couldn't even look at the older of the two brothers. How many times had I dreamed of a man looking at me in such a way? A man who would punish me in all sorts of ways. A man who—

Now he stood directly in front of me. More like he towered over my helpless form. If only I could free my wrists from where they connected to each other behind my back. Caleb may have permitted me to put on my clothes again, but I felt absolutely naked and vulnerable.

"Do you remember what I told you?" he asked. His lips remained slightly parted at a height above my forehead.

He'd said so many things. All dark and threatening. Now, standing so close to me, he tilted my chin upward.

My only response was a shudder.

"I said I was going to fuck you." He said those words sexier than anyone I'd ever imagined. "I said—" he reached the neckline of my shirt "—I was going to rip off your dress." And he ripped the front of my shirt, not stopping until it was torn all the way down the front. Next came the bra, which he easily snapped from the clasp between the cups. Those furious hands went to my jeans. They weren't even cheap jeans, but somehow, he yanked and the button popped off, followed by stress to the zipper.

Would a rip further down the mid seam be possible after? They'd already reacted as though they were nothing more than jeggings.

Yes, they continued to tear all the way past my slit. The panties were the easiest to snap at the gusset. Through all this, he didn't let me look away from his emerald eyes, and every second had my heart racing more and more.

He ungently pushed my thighs apart, exposing my core. For whatever stupid reason, I wanted him to force his lips against mine and demand a fierce kiss when he pushed the remnants of my top down my arms. I wanted him to peel his shirt away so his firm chest connected to mine. His fingernails needed to be digging into the skin of my exposed back as he held me in place.

I must have been drunk on the moment, because I didn't even know he'd freed his cock. Sure, my mind had me loving the possible sensations, but I felt the surprise when he shoved into my tender core, slamming our bodies together.

"This was meant to be mine first," he declared. His cock felt bigger than Caleb's but didn't land too deep.

John didn't bother with being gentle when he fisted the hair at the back of my head. I didn't want gentle. The more dominating, the more passionate and closer to my fantasies. This hadn't gone beyond what I wanted a man to do to me. Not yet, anyway.

I was still at a loss for words. I expected him to be far more terrifying. To unleash his sadist side. Maybe I had this man all wrong. Maybe Caleb wanted me to be at odds with John.

When he'd filled me to the brim, he said, "You knew that before fucking my brother, didn't you?"

Caleb did tell me that John wanted me first. Actually, that John wanted to know the first child was his child. I cringed at the thought. *No.* Babies and breeding weren't part of my fantasies, nor would they ever be.

The hold in my hair tightened as his hips inched backward. He was waiting to kiss me. I knew that by the closeness and his enrapturing gaze. He wanted my answer first, though.

I began, "We—"

"Yes or no." This time, he scooped me by my lower back and pulled me forward more at the edge of the counter. Another plunge into me hit that perfect spot.

"Yes," I breathed. The force of our bodies colliding was surprising, but desirable, no less. Why hadn't I considered this to be a possibility?

He'd been the sort of man I agreed to let take me into the shadows. He laid out his plans the first night and had me eager to accept. Oh, right, it came down to his unwillingness to wrap his dick.

As he pumped into my core, his mouth took ownership of mine. I shouldn't have loved how both brothers felt. This seemed wrong. As though there had to be one good brother and a bad one. And Caleb failed every test of being a bad guy.

I moaned. Not only because of how good this felt, but every thought of the pleasures to come. They could both have me in a repeating cycle if it would feel this good.

The kiss became so fierce that by the time our lips separated, I had to catch my breath. He had no desire to make oxygen an easy feat, and his mouth latched to mine again as his pistoning grew more impassioned. Really, *really* impassioned. The sort of impassioned after a woman finally submitted to the man who owned her. The way an alpha male claimed what belonged to him. Like when the bandit captures a Virgin princess—

The next plunge into me had me bobbed backward with him achingly deep. Fuck, did his gorgeous emerald stare own my soul as hot seed burst into me.

He held in place, breathing against my face, examining my desperate expression for fulfillment. And he appeared livid, given the amazing sex we'd just experienced. "You were thinking about someone else." He spoke matter-of-factly.

My heart crashed downward. Technically, I was merely comparing it to similar experiences I'd longed for. There was no particular man on my mind. Certainly no one I had been with prior to John, who brought all those past fantasies of impassioned sex to my mind.

His manhood pushed uncomfortably deeper and twitched against my cervix, freeing whatever seed remained. "Next time I'll make certain you're not able to imagine anyone but me while I breed this pussy I own." The sadist-turned-impassioned-lover flipped back to being a hostile sadist.

I didn't know how to respond. I knew he'd stated his intentions to end my joyful life by making me a mother. That wasn't an option. It also helped me to get back into the mindset of not being dragged away by these two irresistible brothers who came close to feeling like real-world fantasies, if not for the breeding fetish plans.

After a step backward and jerking his pants up, he pulled my arm to bring me to rise from the counter. If only Caleb were close by, I wouldn't be as concerned by the ungentleness. But Caleb would only add another person I would need to escape. Running from Caleb would be fun and rewarding. A run from John, though.

I cringed at the thought. Why hadn't I trusted my instincts and gotten away earlier?

Now I would have no choice but to seek protection from cops. That in itself would be a disappointment, but the brothers could always be in my mind, awaiting their opportunity and watching me. So long as it didn't come to being ensnared again, I could settle for that outcome.

When John began toward the door with me in tow, I attempted to twist my arm free. "At least give me your shirt or jacket." Remembering his delight with flowers, I grabbed a vase of two dozen long-stemmed crimson roses. "And I need flowers."

He didn't release me, and his narrowed eyes reminded me of my lack of rights to make demands. "You don't deserve clothes." His grip on my upper arm tightened. "Walk fast if you don't like being cold." Those words preceded him speedily forcing me out of my shop.

The temperature was in the low fifties, and he expected me to go out there topless and crotchless, with cum dripping down my thighs. Sure, in a fantasy, being subjected to torturous conditions could be fun, but not like this when I actually had to experience the discomfort.

His urgency led us beside the pond in less than a minute. Tossing Caleb in seemed mean and foolish. Kinky in the punishment, but I didn't want to do it. Knocking John in seemed more along the lines of survival from what horrors would come to me in the looming touring vehicle's silhouette ahead.

Nope. The brothers were obviously wealthy, given that was what he arrived in and decked out with a dungeon. They didn't know the area well enough to catch up to me if I ran.

With John's focus on getting me to the vehicle that equated to my doom, I clung to my flowers and faked a trip, so he had no choice but to stop. The successful attempt had him stopping to force me up, at which point I hastily swung the heavy vase at him. He had to free me to block it, giving me the opportunity to also push him sideways to drop into the frigid pond that sat perfectly low enough.

He could experience the shock of the cold. And he fell, just as I hoped. Not all the way in, since it wasn't completely full, but into a few feet and the slippery clay that wasn't easy to get out of.

And I knew better than to give him another glance, so I ran.

Dirty

D^{*on't look back.*}

on't look back.

Those words repeated in my mind. And why the hell wasn't I running toward the tree-line? Why was I running toward the massive touring bus and my house? At the realization and the unsteadiness taking hold, I turned to run into the field toward a neighboring house only a quarter of a mile away. The elderly couple could help me.

Lights weren't on to guide my footing, but I grew up here. Even in my teenage years, I longed for the need for escape from home invaders or nords that came to capture women. Sexy shirtless men who stopped at nothing to have me—and they would surely rip off my clothes and demand my submission once I'd been captured.

The thought gave me a new energy, but unlike those wild desires to be owned, I couldn't fall to the ground and scurry backward with a man catching up to tower above me. Those nords were nice in my memories. They did things that would make any girl desperate for release.

Halfway there.

Flashes overtook my mind. Years' worth of memories of all the ways my imagination said such a run would end. Excitement to see a line of men, all of whom were ready to claim me. My heart pounded, not permitting me to hear my own feet hit the hard dirt or anything around.

Then came the force from behind that had me with my face and nude chest planted to the cold ground. And then the teenage day-dreams consumed me. Why the fuck did he have to land on me in a way that easily positions him to have his way with my body? To easily use his manhood to mark me as his and roughly use me with the sort of force that would break my will to fight. Out of fantasy habit, my legs spread wide, baring my exposed core.

Water leaked down onto me, and the cold of wet clothes stuck to my back. His groin pressed downward, though not as hard as I would have imagined. "If you think this little act of submission is going to save you from my wrath, you are mistaken, slave." Each word came out with a sharpening growl.

The cold and his recent use of my body hindered him from fulfilling one of my darkest desires.

"I should have put you in your place the moment I had you alone." He placed a firm grip on my wrists with his weight baring down.

I'd been here before. Whimpering beneath a man who planned to do the most tormenting of things to me. Unfortunately cold and uncomfortably held with a heavy weight crushing me. But that only added to the intensity of this shocking moment.

"You're hurting me." I forced as deep of a breath as I could.

Cold water still dripped from his hair onto me. He lifted his weight that had squeezed me, but he didn't rise. "You have no fucking idea what pain feels like."

And I believed his threat. "Please. Let me up." I just wanted him off. I wanted warmth. Even if I'd failed to get free, he could provide me with a small amount of comfort instead of this. The richer billionaire or mafia types never would consider keeping their captive in the mud.

He preferred to torture me over getting himself warm. Couldn't he at least care about his own comfort? A man who would endure cold and misery to make me suffer worse would be a horror to be owned by.

"You'll get sick." I hoped the feigned concern would work. After all, the guy liked flowers and classical music. He wanted someone romantic and caring for his well-being.

"If you cared about that, you wouldn't have tossed me into a filthy fucking country water hole."

He had a point, but why was he arguing? This was my dark and brooding captor. In no well-reviewed book I read did people behave outside of expectations. And his inconsistency made me doubt everything about him.

It wasn't like I was the unreliable narrator of my own life. I saw things precisely as they were. Except for when I thought about the dark antiheroes and billionaire kidnappers I so loved. And maybe the way I bumped into men at night with certainty they would drag me to their shifter lair of five men who all wanted me.

If only I hadn't become too cold and shivery for the excitement of the thought.

John had acted wolfish. I knew paranormal wasn't real, but maybe he was simply a bit of an alpha type that was also loving. Puppyish and playful and unconcerned with the cold.

"I'm going to punish you beyond belief," he hissed against my ear.

And shifters made for fun disciplinarians.

Once again, I found myself saying the foolish word that I said the night we met. "Okay." Ridiculous, of course. No one would actually say that in this predicament. But what else would I do? Fighting this wouldn't work. "But no breeding."

His words came out in a growl. "I'll spend all night filling you with my cum, slave." And with those words, his weight and the wetness of his clothing no longer pressed onto me. "But I'm not going to fuck a woman who's probably covered with cow shit."

Countryness

I t truly was more than an RV that we approached—with me shivering the entire walk toward it. It seemed to be sized similar to one of those sports team touring buses that had plenty of room for a group to live in for a brief time. I imagined the Subaru could drive up into the back. It probably still would only take a third of the length space and have plenty of room above it.

A queasiness set in. I wouldn't escape the brothers. But maybe some of John's behaviors and what Caleb had told me earlier would prove the older brother nicer than how he'd been acting.

Some antiheroes were warm beneath their harsh exteriors. Most likely, John was one of them. I didn't want to go into this bus with any other belief.

"Your house first to wash the countryness off," John snapped.

Countryness? A guy who could afford a touring bus had a problem with a little rural dirt on him? I recalled Caleb's warning about John having OCD. Now I worried a bit about what being considered clean might entail. It wasn't like I'd actually fallen in manure.

Once in my house, I flicked on the lights, shifting a side eye to John, who appeared caked with mud, wet and sticky, and absolutely fuming about it. If I hadn't been so miserably cold and mostly naked aside from the tight legs and rear of my jeans, I might have laughed. If he'd been Caleb, the sight would receive a snicker. But not John. John wasn't the sort I trusted to tolerate laughter.

"Turn on the shower," he ordered, grabbing my wrist when I reached for my coat. He released me and peeled off his drenched shirt.

Damn, he looked good. Like the sort of dirty sexy of an alpha of a motorcycle gang. Greasy and dirty, but in just the right way.

He ran a hand through his short, mud-streaked hair. And that made him even more sexy until he attempted to shake off the crud that came out. When my attention returned to his stubbly face, his teeth bared. Before he could get any words out, I bolted toward the bathroom.

I had the hot water blasting by the time he followed me in. My teeth chattered as I looked past myself in the mirror to where he'd arrived in the cramped space.

"Hot water takes a sec." I covered my dirty chest with my arms.

"Undress," he demanded.

I looked downward and kicked off my shoes and socks and wiggled out of the torn jeans. My favorite pair.

He'd destroyed the jeans I absolutely loved. I could have left them behind without a thought, but actually taking the opportunity to look at a favorite garment in this condition would make any self-respecting girl cry.

I rathered torture to seeing them so shredded. And despite the brutality they'd suffered, I lovingly folded them and placed them on the counter. A pathetic farewell, but it would have to do.

I turned to watch John step into the small shower, not bothering to close the yellowed curtain. Brown water flowed off of his defined muscles. How the fuck had I thought I could outrun someone of his fitness? And why didn't he ravish me to assert his dominance when he had me on the ground?

Just the thought had my cold, dirty body anticipating the punishment to come. He might do any number of things to me.

"Get in," he ordered, pulling me out of my entranced stare.

I'd been standing here repulsively dirty, gawking at his glorious form. I felt a bout of *instalove* overcome me. I might have always enjoyed the trope, but it was too far-fetched for most people. But they probably had really shitty lives and a pitiful imagination. Or simply knew the truth of inevitable dating failure due to their bitchy attitude and the obsessive need to complain, which could never get a man's cock up.

"*Get. In.*" This time he enunciated, and I realized I'd been staring at the manhood that pointed upward.

How long had that been going on? Wiser than to dare test his patience any further, I went to the small shower we both would barely fit into.

The cramped space didn't bother him. He went to work scrubbing me as though I were a furry pet covered with grime. "I'm going to shave this pussy."

I'd never considered shaving a personal slave as something to bring arousal to a man. I was okay at keeping things well-trimmed. "I can groom it myself." I would maintain a little dignity through the jab at my appearance.

I'd only thought there was too little space in the shower before he closed in on me. My back pressed to the wall, and he braced his left elbow to the side of my head. Water dribbled down from his chin to mine.

"You do whatever the fuck I give you permission to do." His right hand went down to my folds, which were wet with something more than soap and misting water. "And I want it bare, so every time I walk past where you're kept, I see it weeping to be fucked."

Kept? Why was I so mental that the way he said kept sounded sexy? Like the women kept in one area and only visited when they were to be fucked.

And that always had the twisted intent of breeding.

No thanks, creepy dude.

Suddenly *kept* didn't feel so sexy, no matter how dreamy the glossy man was who'd trapped me against the tile. Or the way his fingertips spread and explored my nethers.

His long digits probed. "I like it when you tremble like a scared little bunny."

What was I supposed to say to that? The tremble he mentioned also took hold of my voice. "Thank you."

As he dedicated his hand to my body, he watched my every response. Not in the *I want to provide you with pleasure* sort of way. This careful assessment seemed more in tune with figuring out how to exploit my body's reaction to his touch. And I always loved the way a captor in a forced proximity novel had his slave begging for him.

The way he could look at her and have her heart-rate pulsing. The way the graze of his knuckles, even against the forearm, could make his hungry gaze a treasure. And now, these piercing green eyes behind a dark line of thick wet lashes threatened to affect me in such a way. If only his intentions didn't include children, I could drink in every millisecond of his attractiveness.

The intensity of his focused gaze created an internal turbulence I wasn't ready to deal with. I attempted to look past him to the rusty showerhead.

"Look at me," he demanded, continuing his exploration that captured my most sensitive area with the friction of his stroke.

It was a shameful thing to look into the eyes of a man whose craving could be so overwhelming. A man I knew had jacked off to the image of me before ever planning to capture me. He'd probably fantasized about this moment of me being cornered every time he considered turning me into his property.

Now that I knew he came from wealth, I needed to gain the courage to ask about my worth. "How much did I cost you?" Hopefully, more than thirty thousand, excluding the expense of hiring me, travel, and purchase of all the flowers from multiple states.

Deep breaths swelled his shimmery body. Rage seemed to billow, as though a fire from within him caused the steam. "You didn't put a dent in my finances."

I supposed that could be good or bad. Either I'd been really cheap for a purchasable person or he didn't have to keep track of his finances in the least. Preferably the latter. After all, this man didn't have a small dick, and he didn't need to draw attention to himself by flaunting wealth.

The closer he leaned so his head hovered inches above mine, the more water streamed down from his face. With his hand no longer exploring me, he raised his arm, positioning so his elbows were above my shoulders to either side of my head.

His cock pushed against my stomach, both promising to fulfill my darkest desires and warning of torment to be inflicted. "I would fuck you now, but since you're so worried about how much you're worth, we might as well save that fun for the fancy, high-priced new equipment I bought to punish you."

Water may have been pouring down, but my eyes widened, unconcerned with the spray. My lips may have parted, but no words would find their way out.

"And we should probably get on the road to pick up the additional items I had to special order after you chose to run away." He had this sort of sexiness of an islander drenched from a waterfall, ready to claim me beneath the waters he ruled over.

My voice didn't even sound like my own when I said, "Okay."

The Tour Bus

Did he like my response? How long could a man tower in such a provocative way without the intention of ravishing me? It felt like those times when I got all excited about swoon-worthy antiheroes who decided they were the sorts to only fade to black. And I'd already gotten my hopes up, only for him to gather the shampoo to wash my hair. Then he directed me out, dried me and himself off, found a set of *his* clothes already waiting on my table, and ordered me—while I was still nude—to follow him out to his touring bus.

Even if I wanted to run, which I didn't care to fail at again, my bare feet wouldn't let me. I had to hobble over the gravel to the looming vehicle. That had its own sexy brooding vibe in my helplessness.

A motorized door opened near the front. Bright light didn't come pouring out as I would've expected. It was a crimson color that provided hellish guidance inside.

"Get in." His order held a lesser amount of irritation, most likely due to the low instrumental music Caleb may have turned on to calm the older brother's rage. Unless that music had already been on.

Now then, onward into the bowels of their mysterious ship to see what this arrogant man of excessive wealth believed I deserved to be punished with. As I took the step past him, I saw the flash of his satisfaction at his win. But a long, calming inhale I took reminded me of how many times I fantasized about such a dooming walk.

Sure, there weren't a bunch of sexy nords or shifters all waiting to use me, but I could still pretend. I could imagine every man from the masquerade awaited as I drew into the lair of hauntingly beautiful music. Every step felt as though a cello laid out the pieces of the crimson world before me. As though it began to expand and become my sandbox dungeon. Larger on the inside. Near magical and unending, as though a superior race of aliens had beamed me to their ship to force me away to be theirs for eternity.

Though, reality set in again after I took the few steps up and turned left. Several vases of flowers greeted me. They must have been Caleb's effort to calm the beast currently tight behind me, which was most certainly endearing. But where was Caleb now?

John breathed deep from behind me, but I wasn't certain if the fresh smell and red-tinted blooms blocking the path further were responsible. He nudged me forward, past the deceptively welcoming long-stemmed flowers; but they undoubtedly hid something horrid from clear view.

The springy floor warmed my cold soles as I stepped forward, pushing past the several tall gladius blooms that curved into the path. Beyond it proved to be an area that had two metal poles that reached the ceiling. One in the center and one close to the dark wall that must have been a tinted window.

The one near the wall held a bit more lighting in a pinkish hue shining over Caleb, who sat with his legs extended, reading a book.

Why he chose that spot instead of the dark couch that stretched the other wall seemed strange.

"I'm not a stripper," I muttered low, trying my best to cover my chest and nether regions.

"Stripping involves someone who gets clothes," John retorted.

Caleb tossed the book down, beaming. "I don't know, clothes aren't too bad. I love the way the vampire in this book captures her and rips off her clothes."

Thankfully, the beta didn't see my blush when I saw the cover of what he currently read. The memory of that passage, which I'd read time and again, had me tensing at the fantasy. The way I escaped the castle in the luxurious Victorian dress. The way the vampire's body slammed me down to the ground. His claws all but shredded the dress as I squirmed to get free from beneath him. Every inch forward was several inches of fabric sliced free until he'd fully exposed my back, and he gripped my waist to pull me onto hands and knees before his massive cock plunged into me.

In hindsight, that would have been a wonderful thing for John to have done when he had me laid out beneath him. What a memory that would have been. I turned my head to look upward over my shoulder at the grumpy man who'd chosen not to give me a splendid memory to feast on. Though, the cold and dirt that made its way into my mouth at that time wouldn't have made it anything worth thinking fondly of. At least now I could imagine he'd fucked me with fury in that field, shoving my face to the ground as his manhood pulsed into me and his weight fell on my body.

I may have been shivering from the cold and shame of my nudity, but heat throbbed in my core. Excitement stirred by such a threat seemed foolish. I hadn't a doubt he noted my response to him by the sternness of the stare cast down, causing me to return my attention to Caleb.

"Help set up," John snapped, bumping my arms as he moved past me to the couch on my left.

Caleb's gaze roved my nude form I'd attempted to hide with my hands. "I'll be the one to catch you next time." He teasingly winked before standing, still gripping the steamy book.

"There is no next time." John seemed certain of his ability to keep me locked away in this touring bus. It hadn't appeared like the dungeon I'd been led to believe, but when he pulled the armrest from the couch and guided the two legs beneath it effortlessly like it was on invisible rails beneath the soft flooring, my opinion of the seemingly harmless area changed.

Caleb came over to me, lowering to cuff my ankle with one of the soft restraints like he'd used on my wrists.

John only glared as he raised the cushioned device to near hip height. The end perfectly lined up between the poles, and the cuffs being placed on my ankles made me realize exactly what he planned to use it for.

I'd read about the ways Masters would restrain their personal fucktoys with legs spread wide to such punishment benches. And those poles had been perfectly distanced for my ankles to be immobilized far apart.

They weren't the sort of books I would buy, just the free short stories on kink websites. Not to being lashed while immobilized or fucked with roughness. It wasn't something I even cared to imagine.

"Caleb," I whispered. Would he save me from his brother? He looked up at me while fastening the cuff.

"Yeah, beautiful?" His warm beam suggested everything would be fine.

I only had enough time to open my mouth, but John's deep voice hindered my ability to speak.

"Over here, slave," he ordered, "now." He waited beside the narrow bench that seemed to have lengthened.

Now I wished I'd tried harder not to be captured. I could have refused Caleb earlier and then been safe.

"Pony up, Jules!" Caleb said as he rose again.

I shook my head, desperately covering myself a bit more with my hands to feel safer. "I'm not getting on there." As always, I'd been too bold. I knew what happened to the captives who talked back. And pain wasn't something my feeble body cared for.

"Now, slave." John didn't even use the hostile tone this time, but I remained frozen to the spot, with Caleb shielding me.

Caleb whispered, "Just be a good girl for me, so he won't use the flogger."

The Mobile Dungeon

The dooming punishment device awaited me like a miniature pummel horse. Swiftly leaving it, John returned to the couch, raising the seat to reveal the underside could tilt upward and held an assortment of punishment devices.

I took the three steps to the bench, hopeful John wouldn't reach for the flogger, the narrow black paddle, or the short cane. If he chose nothing but used his hand, I would be relieved.

He didn't even have to ask me to bend onto the bench. I already knew to do so. I also knew to spread my legs until my outer ankles were against the adult-themed poles.

Caleb quickly responded to that and connected their fasteners into outward bulges of metal from small rings at the bottoms of the metal poles.

John waited, watching me while I remained in the position. The bench wasn't even long enough for me to rest my head. I knew better than to complain, though, since he had the power to make this situation more uncomfortable if he chose to.

This was my new life, at least for now. And John was nothing like the dark stories where I could imagine myself in a similar position splayed before some sexy stranger in all black who planned to mercilessly ravish me. If only he'd been wearing a suit to make him like one of those billionaires who purchased me to be his well-behaved, submissive wife.

He remained delicious as sin as he arrogantly sauntered my way with a black paddle as his choice weapon of pain. I didn't want this, but my ankles were cuffed and connected to the bottoms of the poles. The brothers had bound me in a way that I was helpless and couldn't attempt to escape.

I struggled to say his name. "J–Joh—"

His eyes narrowed, silencing my stutter.

Don't speak, just remain silent. The books did this so much better in the safety of my home or in the dark, as my phone screen let me fantasize about these moments. But now, fantasy had become a nightmare.

He reached beneath my neck, pulling a section from the bench, which extended a small, cushioned section, which he then twisted sideways and raised a few inches and clicked into place as a rest for my chin.

I submitted and looked downward to the floor with my chin pressed to it. Maybe if I said nothing else and behaved like a good slave, the pain wouldn't come.

Vampires. Think about vampires. Love the things they would do to me if they had me. The way they could run cool hands—

John grabbed one of my cuffed wrists and brought it to the bottom side of the chin rest, snapping it into place. He knew exactly how to nightmarishly draw this out, taking far too long to adjust the connection before doing the same with the other wrist.

Pressure teased at my slit.

My imagination? No. That had to be Caleb's doing.

I sucked in a breath of relief. He easily made being owned feel like a fantasy. The gentleness of the strokes found more moisture than should have been possible, given my current unease.

"Oh, baby girl, you are so turned on right now." Caleb kissed the back of my thigh as the pads of his fingers teased my most pleasurous spot.

Just me and him. I was with a man who wanted to indulge my darkest desires—

"This is punishment!" John snapped.

"Mmmm-hmmm." Caleb's hum trailed up my inner leg; his tongue replacing the fingers that had felt so marvelous.

Just me and Caleb. Just Caleb here to sate my desire. Oh God, did his warm tongue feel amazing as it lapped against me, bringing my every muscle to relax. He was the viking who planned to make me his for the rest of my life. To be forever at the mercy of his insatiable desire to worship my passion for him.

It must have been the tip of John's paddle that landed on my shoulder and slowly dragged along my spine, consistent with his slow steps on my left.

Focus. Tune out John. It's just Caleb with me.

Or maybe Caleb was biding his time to please me before defeating the villain readying to break us apart. What was John but the antagonist who would block all joy just as he'd blocked my orgasm earlier? The one eager to take away the gratification Caleb most certainly promised.

My beta didn't have concern in the least. His lips wrapped the bundle of nerves, maybe in response to my slight rocking that bid him to angle more as I felt the ache continue to rise. The need to find release slowly teasing its way to the surface.

As my want built, the weight of the paddle rested on my lower back. Thankfully, this increasingly let me enjoy Caleb's efforts to please me, knowing that the device was no longer a threat.

A fingertip twirled around my left nipple, warm and moist, creating the sort of tingle that rapidly fueled the building orgasm. Caleb's ability to satisfy a captive woman rivaled any creature or being I'd fantasized about—and those dark desires were shamefully more numerous than I cared to admit.

A mix between a moan and whimper escaped me as he slowed the teasing motions of his tongue.

"I want you to know something, slave." John kneeled beside me, forcing my awareness to his finger that twirled my areola.

My wide eyes stared downward, but I could also see much of his crouching form in my periphery. At least he continued the gentle touches that accompanied Caleb's dedication to my pleasure.

"My baby brother doesn't want to cause you pain, so he knows the importance of not bringing that sweet climax you are so desperate for." His voice raised as he continued, "Right, brother?"

Caleb's mouth lowered.

No, no. no. Let me be punished. Don't stop after bringing me so close. I needed this release after all I'd been through. I needed my beta willing to make me feel good, even if it cost me dearly.

John could go be an asshole somewhere else and leave me and Caleb to enjoy ourselves.

"Caleb," I whimpered.

"Hmmmmm, baby girl?" Caleb's wet lips tickled my inner thigh, kissing and blowing warmth against me. "You know I want to keep you happy." He nipped my leg.

"Go help navigate out of this hell-hole." John's order was followed by the departure of Caleb's touch and, most certainly, him leaving the area. So, the alpha John did have his loyal beta. But alphas could be challenged. Especially when an omega suffered the tyrannical alpha's abuses.

The throb between my legs didn't subside, not with the way this alphahole continued to toy with my breast. Torment. This was the sort of wrongness against a damsel that my Caleb wouldn't tolerate forever. Of course, right now, John was my only hope for relieving this overwhelming desperation for an orgasm.

I panted, desperate for more than simple teases to my nipple. "Please, John."

Had I resorted to begging? Abso-fucking-lutely. Would it work? Every passing second made me a bit more fearful he would refuse. Especially when he stole his massaging fingers from my sensitive breast.

He huffed. His timbre had a sadistic husk. "What sort of Master would I be if I didn't correct your misdeeds?" The weight of the paddle lifted from my lower back. His voice hardened a bit, and he enunciated his next words. "Every single one of your misdeeds."

It felt as though the music I'd tuned out increased, though maybe this more sinister tempo resonated with the mood.

John continued, "Including your disrespectful way of addressing me."

This was the part that could have any girl panting long past her normal waking hours. And John was the sort of dark and dominating man who could rile a needy woman's core to the point of no return. Ebbing with a warning sound of whatever classical piece played. But not like this. I couldn't desire this to truly occur. Not when certain pain stalked, intending to add angst to this slowly unfolding horror.

I tilted my head up and looked over my shoulder to the towering alpha, who stroked a fingertip over the edge of the paddle he studied.

He shifted his shoulders with a notable hitch. The same sort of hitch of a musician about to beckon his cello into position before playing.

A flash of him in his suit took hold of my mind. He'd looked amazing in that suit. And the only thing sexier than a man in a suit is a man whose fingers are caressing a cello.

"Cello..." I breathed. Was I biding time? Or did he drag out a sort of hunger I'd never gotten to feast upon in all my fantasies?

John's eyes narrowed, and the tip of his forefinger outlined the rounded end of his paddle again.

He'd claimed I showed disrespect, so maybe a better way of addressing him would work in my favor. "Sir."

How convenient the moment of forgiveness would be at the brink of crescendo.

No such luck. His expression didn't calm, and he reared back with the cruel device of punishment.

"Master." I squirmed against the restraints holding me in place, futile though I knew it to be. I would call him whatever the fuck he wanted in order to prevent agony. *"God!"*

Doom. That was all I heard and saw and sensed. A black paddle lashing out at my sensitive rear. He timed it perfectly, so the sound and fiery pain collided with the cruel music that came from every direction.

"Sir will suffice." His blazing eyes met mine.

In truth, he looked very much a demon in hell's destructive glow. But did the devil himself harness such a love of melody? The sort of love that had him strumming the end of the paddle before the innately natural moment of melodic despair to raise the instrument of my suffering again.

I quivered through the radiating agony. *"The cello...Sir."*

A pause. The hesitation forced him to miss his moment. Only seconds left before he might strike.

"You play." I struggled for a dreadful breath. Fearful of his next strike. "Will you?"

His tongue roved side to side over his lower lip as thoughts played on his expression. Now even his breath held attunement to the strings that quaked the air.

Music calmed him. *Pachelbel's Canon in D.* Every cellist loved that one. The flow and adoration within it. The love and hope. The way it made flowers appear brighter, feel softer, and even smell sweeter.

"Canon in D, Sir," I begged.

It didn't take a book for me to fantasize about a groomsman whenever I heard the piece. Not that a florist could ever actively fraternize with the guests. We were to be invisible, making my imaginary capture all the more fun. Unnotable, shy, helpless to even hear the steps from behind as I hummed to the melody. A hand covering my mouth as I was dragged into a dark corner or closet. Ravished passionately to one of the most romantic songs in existence. Always to remember the event every time I heard the musical piece. Embarrassed when I stumbled out disheveled after having attempted to gain my composure. My trembling legs would lead me out into a world of men in tuxes, and I may not even know which one had me. I might only know by the brooding and arrogant stance of a smug male across the room.

But for it to be a performing cellist himself to be the one to have his way with me—

Pain. Fiery-hot, popping loud as though a cannon blast. My focus blurred. I couldn't see. I couldn't think. I only felt the torment of the paddle that landed. A second, and then a third, and then a fourth time.

My cries didn't even sound as though they were my own. They seemed distant, like the woman who'd been dragged away into a closet, coming from somewhere. Muffled.

"I've looked forward to hearing you cry every moment I spent sound-proofing this dungeon after your poor attempt to escape me."

Had he just spoken? That wasn't my imagination.

Happy place. Happy place. Where the fuck was my happy place?

Another powerful smack landed on my already cruelly victimized backside.

"And I warned you that you wouldn't be thinking of anyone but me." He lashed out at me with the paddle several more times until the ache radiated down the backs of my thighs.

Even if I could have come up with words, I couldn't speak through the rolling sobs. I couldn't see through the pinkish blur of my fat tears. So help me God, I would never read another dark romance for the rest of my life. If I escaped this asshole, I'd just suffer the miserable boredom of whatever clean crappy literature flashed before my eyes in the ads.

"Do I have your attention yet?" the cocky asshole asked.

Did he really just ask whether he had my attention?

He had my backside in a state of eternal flame. Of course he had my attention. Even biting my lower lip didn't halt the quiver. All I could manage was a weak nod in response to his ridiculous question.

Where was Caleb? Why hadn't he overthrown his tyrannical alpha brother? Why the fuck had I even stupidly got lost in the lure of the younger brother's charms that left me vulnerable to John's sadism?

Pressure landed on my inflamed backside. John's hands, maybe? The throb remained, even if the pressure felt nice. "Next time won't be this gentle."

Gentle? He thought that absolute torturous pain was gentle? I still had no way to respond as I hovered in shocked awareness. Even as he massaged the area.

I didn't need a fucking massage! "Caleb." I struggled through a sob. Caleb could be the one to comfort me after this brutal paddling.

John continued to stroke the angry flesh. "This isn't a playground I set up for children."

Was he claiming Caleb acted like a child? Or both of us?

Forgive us for the decade we lagged behind the oh-so-wise and pretentious jerk. Not like I could speak my mind on the matter. I couldn't hold my lips steady or even mute my whimpers.

The kneading sensation continued, but migrated closer to my core. My responding jolt was met with him shushing me and fingertips pressed to my entry. His exploration located the bundle of nerves that hadn't lost the need from when Caleb worked his magical tongue on me.

I hated this asshole for all he'd already done. Worse, I hated him for thinking he could continue the action where Caleb had been forced to stop pleasuring me. Why would this alphahole reap the rewards of—

Those cello fingers strummed my most pleasurous spot. There was no other way to describe whatever he just did.

"Caleb," I said again, just as weak as the last time.

John's response came with a soft swirling against my pulsing nub. It should have been reacting to the absolute agony of my backside as opposed to his touch.

"The only man you're going to be thinking about right now is me," he said.

He'd certainly mastered hindering any thoughts aside from my agony-ridden body. Right now, he also had me very aware of his melodious touch. A sensation I needed to hate, especially as his member pressed at my slick entry.

Why was I so receptive? This man had just caused me the most pain I'd ever experienced. He made sure this traveling dungeon was decked out in a way that guaranteed my torment. He'd plotted and purchased me for no specified amount—

His manhood sank into me hilt deep; his body against my angry flesh. And his finger continued its perfected strumming.

"Fuck," he breathed, hardly audible over the classical piece that just began to play. A slow one.

He chased me down in a field, miserably cold, with no top and shredded jeans—

He inched out of me before a steady glide into my depths again, swirling desire and pain through me as they battled for my attention.

He paddled me! Caused me to cry—

"Who's fucking you, Julie?"

I lingered in a mix between loving the sensation and hating this over-the-top alpha male who demanded my attention.

His lean forward pressed his weight onto my back, his lips against the hair over my ear. "Who's fucking you?"

"You are," I replied.

Of course he demanded my full attention. His next shove into me held more force, though easily glid into my welcoming slickness. Pleasing, despite my pained backside. Bliss inducing.

Should I add in all the things the mafia bosses wanted to hear? All the things that I so desperately fantasized about? Did I dare think of the random man with short messy blond hair?

Not if I wanted this bizarrely amazing bliss to surface. "Sir."

"Fuck, Julie." His grind had this way of adding friction to that perfect spot inside me. His strumming ended, his hands preferring to find my breasts, adding to the rapidly growing need.

The pumping into me stopped. "Your pussy should be milking my cock with a soul-shattering orgasm." His grip added a painful squeeze to my nipples.

He planned to do this to me again? To refuse me the gratification of the ache he'd caused. Of what Caleb had stirred. Reversing everything. And all the pained sensations mixed with his voice didn't let me go to that happy place where my mind could easily let this come on its own.

This torment felt far different when enjoyed in a book. To be read over and over again with anticipation. But to experience it. Oh, how I loathed him. Not the way he slammed into me. I loved that, but it had the sort of angle that ignored the heavenly location that would have sent me into bliss.

"You've been bad, Julie."

Whispered from him in such a tone, my name gave me a high. Maybe he would let me find my release. Maybe—

"Julie," he groaned, shoving hilt deep, blasting into me. He remained in place, ensuring I didn't receive the friction I needed. Instead, the throb of the sting on my rear took hold.

The monster! The fucking bastard!

"Every fucking day I spent miserably away from you will be multiplied before you earn any orgasm."

He may have been wealthy as fuck, but the billionaires always made certain the woman they purchased or forcibly married received soul-shattering pleasure. This man had the abusive manner of the villains in the twisted romances I didn't dare explore.

Unending Fantasies

I never cared to hear all those annoying details that made the pacing suck. Yeah, John freed me from the bench. He also placed an ice pack to my core until I became too numb. Then he let me have a few minutes of privacy to take care of business and rinse the area off.

And now? Now I had a two-foot-long chain attached to my ankle cuff that kept me securely connected to the metal pole in the center of the space. No bench. Only a couch I couldn't reach. Not even clothing aside from a black chastity belt. It didn't look monstrous. It was simple, with a heart shape in the front and bendable but tight straps. However, the area of my core had a wide silver swell that ensured no friction.

And he did ensure I craved release before securing it to me. Before he left, he said, "I know you were wanting to hear Canon in D, so here you go." And the classical wedding piece played on loop for around thirty minutes before the place went silent and an amber glow replaced the reddish lighting.

Finally, Caleb stepped in and came to my rescue. Not that he could do anything for me. John had me under lock and key.

Caleb's lower lip tucked between his teeth as he snuck over to me with an arm suspiciously hidden behind his back. He looked so breathtaking in a black tee and loose pants. So relaxed, yet swoon-worthy. And the way his hair flowed down to his shoulder made him all the more handsomely exotic.

"I brought you something." He lowered to sit in front of where I sat with my back against the metal dancer's pole and my arms crossed in front of my chest.

I couldn't decide whether I wanted to glare at him or accept the gift box he extended to me. But how could I hate the hero? The one who, when chance arose, would free me of his brother. My dark and rugged knight who'd fallen for me despite any oath that would be broken.

When I freed one hand to accept it, he beamed like a teenager with a crush. I lifted the lid, revealing purple fabric.

"I *may* have read one of the books you took with you to the masquerade," he mused.

When I pulled out the sheer purple fabric, a thin gold band also came into view. There were two pieces. The one with gold I let flow. A little slave's skirt with long wide strips for front and back that would most certainly reach ankle length. The other must have been a halter type top when twisted into a figure-eight.

How could I be angry with the one person who'd gone out of his way to give me a dress similar to what a woman in one of my favorite novels wore? I couldn't. There would always be time to fight him, to act out my fantasy and eventually escape. But for now, I felt the urge to show my appreciation for his thoughtfulness.

"Thank you, Caleb," I said.

"Stand up." He tossed the box to the side. "I'll help you put it on."

Clutching the fabric to my chest, I rose, slowly, loving the way he scanned me. I hated the chastity belt that hid my core that began to ache for him. No relief would come from the way this man made me feel so sensually powerful.

He didn't rush to his feet. He took his time and scooted onto his knees my way, kissing my inner knee. Not a simple peck either, but letting his tongue lap up whatever treat he must have imagined coated my inner thigh.

I felt as though I were a princess, forced to marry the powerful king of a rivaling kingdom. No...tribe. This man was too rugged for a simple, well-groomed ruler in a tunic. And, for some unknown reason, he wanted this union. *Me*. Attractive and worth the effort to woo.

Worshipped. Fuck, did he make me feel worshipped as his sucks and lapping moved ever-higher. Nothing felt worse than the moment his lips bumped against the dooming chastity belt that marked me as the slave of a dark lord. The one who must be defeated so the magic binding this cruel device would be forever broken.

The fabric fell from my hands as I preferred to feel his silken hair between my fingers. To imagine his rage at the one who'd tormented me and chained me with a power too great to ever break free of.

By the time he'd reached my visibly shivering navel, my short fingernails dug into his scalp, gently tugging him higher to my swelling breasts. I could feel a rugged stubble of his short beard tickle my skin. The heated breaths that grew more impassioned as he explored ever-higher.

His crown fell, loudly clanking against the stone floor. Who knew how long this prison cell would remain barren of guards after that clatter. Or when a dragon might circle the tower that was lit only by a strip of moon that twinkled in his soul-guzzling sea-green eyes.

Now he'd reached my heaving breasts, and I couldn't fight the urge to rip off the detestable tunic separating our bodies.

Yeah, I changed my mind about the tunic. I had to once the crown fell. Once my god-sent hero who glittered in holy white had come.

Ever higher he came, raising his muscular arms as I yanked the heroic garment upward and off him. Desperate for every powerful suck and twirl of his tongue below my chin that had upturned the moment he gripped the hair at my nape.

"Damn, Jules," he breathed, trailing up to my lips. "I already love every single thing about you."

I needed the massive manhood currently poking my navel to be inside me. I ground forward, desperate for any friction against the vile chastity contraption that refused him easy access.

"Ravish me." I spoke the words I loved imagining. The ones that would have a threadbare dress ripped from my helpless body.

"Baby girl," he hummed before pecking my lips.

I already imagined him pounding into me as I raised a leg to curl around him, so his pelvis firmly held me against the pole that imprisoned my other ankle.

"John has the keys." His whisper tormented me. The possessive Alpha would challenge both of us for eternity. "And this." Caleb's fingers lightly brushed where I'd been paddled. But that weak throb felt like a bonus at this point. A pleasuring sort of heat, and the memory of the cruelty I'd endured due to a billionaire's jealousy at the awareness that he could never have my heart.

"Please," I begged. I had no choice but to drop to my knees, casting a helpless glance upward to Caleb. "Master." Forget the sweet guy who came to free me. Why couldn't I be dominated? To find a way to enjoy this situation that had me trapped.

The side of his mouth quirked upward.

"Just a minute, baby girl," he said, quickly sidestepping to retrieve something before tucking a pillow behind my head and neck. The moment he returned in front of me, darkening eyes looked down with hunger.

If I didn't do as he desired, he could shift into a werewolf, and I didn't want that aggression. I yanked down the front of his loose pants and didn't hesitate to take him into my mouth. It was the erection he hadn't alleviated earlier because he awaited the moment he could return to use my mouth to satisfy his wicked cravings.

I clawed at his thighs as I quickly worked, knowing exactly the perfection he expected of me. But I couldn't do as good as he expected, and he would have to teach me a lesson.

A lesson. Any moment now. Punishment for me not moving fast enough. Not sucking. No longer swirling my tongue.

I was a bratty, defiant personal slave.

I glared upward.

Any moment now.

"Bad, bad, girl, Jules," he purred, teasing me before a forward thrust that had my head to the pillow. His fists went to my hair, not painful as they pulled. Just right in the pressure used.

His hips pumped, and his cock met my throat. "Such a bad slave." He glared down at where I looked up to him, desperate to receive my punishment and forgiveness. Even if I spread my thighs and rubbed the cold silver—which I did do—no gratification could ever quite come to my aching core.

Maybe I would forever be unpleasured due to my bratty ways. My upbringing I'd always rebelled against. Desperation for release may only be met with erotic torment.

Now he shifted one hand to grip the pole as he pumped into me, owning my mouth in a way I'd never thought I could love so much.

"Oh, Jules," he breathed, pushing deep to force his seed straight down my throat.

My beta pulled from my mouth, his own ridged chest swelling in a tempo similar to mine. His grin grew, and he winked down while raising his pants.

Something about this charming man proved to match my every fantasy. The safe space that unleashed my imagination as he knew in detail how to elicit the strong emotions that always captivated me.

"We didn't even get to have fun with your slave-girl outfit." He leaned down to pick up the sheer purple fabric.

And once Caleb lowered, the cruel dark lord who'd imprisoned me came into view in the narrow doorway.

Wonderland Master

I lowered my head in shame and fear of the punishment to come, quickly removing my hand from the silver of the chastity device. Why would I care to call this alphahole anything but Master, Lord, or Dark Lord? They were most definitely who he wanted to be in my life.

"If you're done playing back-alley rape while you think I'm sleeping, you should return to the front," John said to Caleb.

My handsome beta sucked between his teeth and grimaced. He'd comforted me at the risk of his own hide. Noble and caring, unlike the cruel Master who'd come to end our affair.

All reality set in as John marched toward us and yanked the fabric from Caleb's clutches. "Give me that," the alpha spat.

I covered my chest, unwilling to give John the satisfaction of an easy peek at my breasts. He pushed past Caleb and squatted in front of me, gripping my ankle as he used his key to unlock the spot where the chain had been secured.

John held me by the upper arm and lifted as though I were a naughty child to be dragged away. He led me further into the back, past the door that entered the moderately spacious bathroom for a tour bus.

After unlocking the next door, we entered a section with black curtains over the walls and a bed with purple silk sheets that took up the entire end. Caleb must have gotten those for me, but I would be stuck with John.

"You're bound to be exhausted, so sleep," he ordered.

"I want to be with Caleb," I muttered, not concerned with any punishment that might follow my insubordination.

John tossed the sheer outfit to the side. "Why? So you can dress up like Princess Honeysuckle or play Pirates of Ravishment?"

That happened to be a very good short story I found online and read on more than a few occasions. He'd gone through my browser history. What a fucking nosy jerk.

John glared down at where my arm hugged around my chest. He truly was a jealous asshole. At least Caleb had moderately warned me.

Embarrassed at the situation and his judgment, I scanned the room, catching sight of a cello on a stand tucked against the corner I'd passed on entry. So he did privately enjoy the instrument, at least enough that it was easily accessible.

"Get on the bed," John ordered.

"Caleb got me those sheets. I don't want to dirty them with you." I immediately struggled to swallow as his eyes narrowed and his teeth bared.

"I ordered those," he said. "And the only reason he knows anything you like is because I paid attention to you."

Caleb did mention John's interest in me. But that was more of a stalker's interest. An obsessed fan who'd seen some of my videos from before my grandmother died and I took over the shop. Back when I'd been a part-time student at the college thirty minutes away as well as helping out at home. I started those occasional videos my freshman year to help make my grandmother's shop known.

Pervert! I couldn't complain too much, though. What girl wouldn't want the attention of a man as sexy and wealthy as him? If he weren't such an asshole, at least.

"Get in the bed," he growled, pressing his body against mine in a way to herd me toward where he wanted me to go.

"Yes, *Master*." My response held venom. He could go ahead and spank me again. It didn't hurt that bad after a while.

"I'm not going to be your wonderland fantasy Master." He continued to steer me toward the bed until I bumped it.

Yeah, no denying it. The thought of him as a wonderland fantasy Master was hot, intentional or not. It felt as though a man I'd been trying desperately to evade for years found me. This time, I wouldn't escape like the several times before. This time, he'd created a special soundproof area in his basement for me. The place he would ravish me time and again on silk sheets.

I collapsed to the bed, helpless on my back to look up at my captor. Fuck, did he turn me on with that dominating glower. I crawled backward, awaiting the moment he gripped my ankle and pulled me to the edge of the mattress to pound into my begging womanhood that couldn't help but answer to his villainous appeal.

My legs spread as I continued further away. Of course I wasn't bidding him to force himself upon me. To rid me of this hindering device that protected me from the certain tormenting pounding as he had me pinned to the bed and forced me to have an orgasm. And what could I do against such power?

The villain worked his dark tee up his body and chunked it to the floor near where the sheer slave outfit rested. Now came the prowl onto the bed; the arrival of his body above mine, his groin pressing against metal that added the hint of pressure to my throbbing nub. I was so helpless against a man with such defined muscles that flexed as he took my wrists and connected the cuffs above my head.

His next reach had the familiar sound of a chain and the click of it locking into one of the wrist restraints. "Are you planning to fantasize non-stop about me giving you the best orgasm of your life?" he asked.

I licked my lips, near breathless to respond. "No, Sir." I hoped he would force it as I fought desperately against the violating pleasure.

"Good." He rolled off me. "Go to sleep." His voice increased with his next words. "Lights off."

The room darkened to inky blackness.

Seriously? He actually did that?

What had I expected, though? This was the asshole that Caleb would free me of. This was the man who'd purchased me because of an obsession.

Banned From Wonderland

Oh, yes, Julie is quite the dreamer in her imaginary wonderland filled with flowers. But she'll settle down soon and run a shop in the big city... and give me some grandbabies as soon as the right man comes along.

They were my grandmother's words in a small local paper interview after I'd drawn attention to her shop with my social media. I thought she could expand since her creations were so loved. And she received more high-paying orders, but further away in the state by clients who did their research when choosing a florist.

Wonderland. She teased me with the word that John used as a weapon. Had he read that article in his time stalking me? Probably.

He'd apparently followed all my posts. They mostly dried up after my grandmother grew ill and completely fizzled soon after her death. He knew all of that, too. Maybe he thought the grandbabies talk was a calling to him as the *right man*.

There was no right man for the baby thing. Though I felt the guilt of never wanting to give her great-grandchildren. After all, she'd practically viewed me as her own child and spoke of me as such. Perhaps she was a bit too indulgent to my fantasies, but not by much.

The alphahole sleeping nearby didn't repulse me as he should have. I'd always cringed at the thought of sleeping with someone. They would've interrupted my thoughts and actions.

John did always interrupt my imagination, and he relished doing so. He also had my wrists bound and pulled up above my head in a way that left me excitedly waiting for more to happen. In a way, this was a fantasy, just a long and boring one that had my mind lingering in a time I'd rather forget about.

Careful as I could, I attempted to turn onto my right side because I also didn't want him waking in a mood to torment me or lash out because of the encounter with Caleb. John hadn't gotten over mine and Caleb's mutual attraction, and I doubted he ever would.

The captor rolled to nestle behind me as a spoon, wrapping a powerful arm over the silk sheet covering me. "Why aren't you sleeping?" he whispered against my neck.

"Because I want to go home."

"No, you don't." He kissed my neck.

"How would you know what I want?" I snapped.

He took hold of my nipple and twisted until I hissed. "Do you want to pay another visit to the bench so soon?"

I swallowed. "No...Sir." The punishment had its appeal if he were to let me find my release. But I knew things might become progressively worse. He was a sadist, after all. Caleb warned me of that much, though I hadn't seen it fully yet. A beast charmed only by music and flowers—an oddly charming requirement.

The hold on my breast loosened, but the kisses on my neck became more firm. That hand tickled its way downward, then fidgeted in his pants pocket before finding its way to the chastity belt.

A soft click preceded the waist straps loosening before the metal pulled from my core, also tugging the rest forward between my legs before the cruel device no longer touched me.

There was no option but to be excited. Then again, I'd spent far too long excited, with no way to alleviate the ache for climax. And minimal options to let my mind wander.

But it could wander now. In this darkness, this person behind me could be any villain, shifter, or even hero. I could have my dominating alpha as I helplessly lay with wrists chained to the wall.

"Lights dim." His order brought a low glow to the room.

So much for imagination. I knew he would expect my absolute engagement with him now.

He soon freed his massive erection from his pants. "On your back," he ordered, growling as though he might shift to a wolf at any moment to assert his dominance over me with fangs.

I already knew to look at him when I rolled onto my back. That had been the reason he demanded the room aglow. But the view of him as he knocked my legs apart and prowled onto me proved the most magnificent sight I'd ever experienced. The glittery green eyes, tousled dark hair, and a hint of stubble. It was a look that topped anything my exhausted mind could conjure, especially when muscular biceps crowded my peripheral vision.

"Wrap your legs around me, Julie."

Easily, he had me obedient to his whims. Maybe it was the way he said my name. I inexplicably loved the way it rolled off his tongue. I always had.

As his tip met my entry, my legs curled around his hips. There was something about his demanding stare that suggested ownership of my soul. The deep plunge that found my cervix before a slow rock backward, only to find it again.

Who wouldn't want such domination from him? Who wouldn't want to look into impassioned eyes of claim or experience strong caging muscles? Nothing could compete with the steady breaths billowing down, or the grind against me that promised satisfaction with every stroke.

He was a merciless ruler who'd laid claim to a woman who strayed too far from home. Binding my arms so I couldn't resist this act of his ownership. An act that might become punishing if I struggled against his rough kiss.

My legs wrapped tighter as I imagined my attempt to scurry from him, uncertain what might happen. This late at night, any beast might roam. He was just a lone shifter who'd captured me, but what if others lined up in wait for their turn?

His next slam into me startled me, forcing my focus to the beautiful face inches from mine. "Do I need to try harder to entertain you, Julie?"

He raised upright, wrapping massive hands around my thighs and pushing them forward so my knees were near my shoulders. From his tower, he looked down at me with possession.

"Who owns you?" he demanded.

"You do—"

His next slam into me sent my eyes wide. I couldn't even say the title he longed for.

"I'm going to make you feel too much pleasure and pain to get lost in your little Wonderland." He pumped forward, grinding in a way that hit that perfect spot and sent currents to my nub. "And I'm going to make sure you crave every minute of what I do to you." Another rock of his hips angled him even more to entice me with the friction.

"And you're going to beg me for release." Now his attention shifted to my nub, and his right hand abandoned my leg to torment me with a pleasurous stroke. A flick of his gaze connected to mine before his focus returned to our joining. "Even when you're swollen with my child, I'll have you mewling for me."

Why the fuck did he have to go there? Babies? His fucking breedmare? *No thanks, pervy captor man!*

My squirm of defiance was met with him slamming forward, so his chest pressed against mine as he began a slow rhythmic pump. The known sadist's forehead rested on mine. "I love how much you love being fucked by me." His mouth crashed to mine, and the thrusts sped.

No matter the position, this alpha knew how to make such a crime feel too good for belief. And even if he'd horrified me with the breeding claims, he made sure to grind in a way I could only seek release.

"You love the way I fuck you, don't you, Julie?" he asked haughtily.

Not that I had to admit anything. I could let him feel powerless to receive my answer until he had no choice but to threaten punishment.

"Does this feel good, Julie? Do you want me to change my mind and let you cum?" No matter how infuriating his arrogance was, he knew my body craved this. He moved slow and passionately in a way I had to respond.

My moans spoke truths I needn't. And my eyes became lost in the unexplored evergreen forests of his stare. Even my fingers longed to sink into his back.

This was no man atop me. This was a God who'd snuck down from the heavens and taken on the most beautiful form. He'd plotted the theft of my innocence with a cock of perfect size and shape. A most powerful being with the goal of bringing forth a holy child to walk the earth.

"Oh, God," I moaned.

"Say my fucking name, Julie!" he said furiously.

He wasn't a God anymore, more like a demon had consumed him. A dark lord and Master. One prepared to pummel my core all the way down to the depths of hell.

I actually preferred that to a ridiculous salvation story.

"Master," I whined, certain of pain to come. Pleasurous pain, certainly eternal in a fiery pit.

With magical speed, he had me flipped onto my front, lifting my rear while keeping my upper body against the silk sheets. A hard smack landed on my backside.

"That's what you called my brother! Say my fucking name, Julie." His feral growl came as another blow landed, sending a sting pulsing throughout my entire rear.

The unimaginative asshole. Sir. Creepy stalker dude. Dark Lord and Monster. Alphahole.

There were times he didn't bother with my name, but times he wanted the address to be personal. Would he want the same for himself?

He felt like an unstable bomb that might annihilate me if I didn't diffuse him.

"John," I cried out.

His body slammed against mine, then pounded furiously as he possessively marked my core as his, and his, alone. Always to be kept in the dark and fiery depths that only he had access to.

A last thrust bottomed against my cervix, pulsing the seed straight into my womb. The promise to make me a mother. Unless he actually had a vasectomy and enjoyed the taunt in the breeding fetish. Though all the billionaires in the stories wanted a specific woman who was theirs to mate with for perfect children.

"Don't ever call me what you call my brother," he said, slowly sliding from me. "Still in that position."

My squirm and attempt to readjust my upper body received a scorching pain to the back of my right thigh. Most likely, a scarlet imprint of his hand remained where the heat clawed at my nerve endings.

Terrified of another session on the bench, I decided it was best to remain in this humiliating position while aching for release.

I did whimper from the agony of that hard smack, and because I couldn't break free of this room. After all, I wasn't permitted to squirm and whimper for freedom from the lair of a possessive dragon.

But this room belonged to John. He had no tolerance for anything but for me to be aware of him. And not the sexy fantasy of an alphahole refusing me an orgasm.

No, that might bring me joy.

Dark Exposure

More and more, I understood Caleb's warnings about John. Sadistic, yes. But not like some psychopaths who enjoyed causing pain. This maniac enjoyed the sort of torment that went deeper than physical punishment.

Instead of bothering to feed me after I groggily woke, John put the chastity belt and sheer slave outfit on me and led me out to the area with the couch and poles. Any items that could be used for torment remained hidden, but that didn't stop my worry about him possibly retrieving one.

"I have a few things I ordered for you that need to be picked up. Caleb will be here soon to feed you. Like a great *Master*." John's tone held contempt for how he'd previously found me submitting to Caleb.

Once John left, I remained standing with my wrists cuffed high to the top of the pole I leaned against. He'd made certain that I couldn't lower onto my knees.

In every way imaginable, John knew how to make my life empty of joy. But that misery somewhat passed after Caleb's return. And he brought food for me to eat. Not to mention, he presented himself as eye candy for me to feast my eyes upon, given he only wore loose beige linen pants.

"I brought your favorite," he said of the spoon of oatmeal he raised to my mouth. "Peaches and Cream." He winked. The man truly was thoughtful, like a gentleman in the books. The charming heroes who knew how to make a woman feel cared about.

Spoon by spoon, he fed me. "I've missed you so much, baby girl." Between bites, he kissed me to taste the sweet flavoring from my lips. "And I brought a secret surprise for my little princess." He placed the bowl on the couch once I'd had my fill.

"A key?" I asked, hopeful for escape—either from the pole or the chastity belt. I wouldn't be picky.

"If only I could get my hands on it. We've got plenty of time for a workaround, though. And there's something I've been wanting to do with you." He went to the side of the bus that didn't have a couch.

The room's soft lighting shifted to purple with a black-light appearance. Next, the sleek black wall opened up, revealing a tinted window, but there were people outside. And large vehicles.

I wasn't exposed, at least. In this lighting, maybe my form could be seen, as well as the interesting glow of the minimalist slave outfit. Soon, my charming beta returned, readying to publicly enjoy my body. We didn't have many options regarding the activities to be performed. Me being the helpless damsel bound with my arms high.

At most, I could only pull against the restraints that had ensnared me. But was he a captor or thief in the night who'd come to steal a kiss? Or even my noble hero, come to try his damnedest to save me.

"I'm about to make you feel so damned good, Jules." Caleb lowered, and I looked to my left out the window to see a few curious forms make their way closer. I didn't know who they were or where we'd stopped. Hopefully, they didn't know anything about me.

As the man who'd come intending to pleasure me dropped onto his knees and lifted my leg, I could only gasp down to his magnificent form. To the topknot I desperately wanted to loosen. To the muscles whose shape I could still make out despite the darkness.

But he could do no more than lift my thigh over his shoulder and kiss it. At least, I thought my bindings would limit him to that sole act until a vibration tickled where his other hand sought entry to the chastity device.

Gorgeous eyes glowed, capturing mine as he pushed the vibration past the silver that blocked my core. Though tiny, it might have been uncomfortable had I not been repeatedly riled and disappointed by John. But Caleb pulled forward yet again, quickly rising to his feet to stand before me.

With a quick scoop beneath my thighs, he lifted me and had my legs spread wide with his abdomen pressing against the chastity belt that now vibrated in a way that had my eyes rolling upward. That wasn't all, though, because my breasts were at level with my impassioned captor's mouth, and he wasted no time locating my right nipple through the sheer material.

He could have freed me. Tossed me down to the floor to my hands and knees and pounded into me from behind, marking me in front of the many citizens of his kingdom. He must have known with certainty that I would run, though. And nothing in this magical world could capture me again were I to escape and land myself in my home realm of goddesses.

Instead, he chose to keep me against this ritualistic post on this holy dais for all to see as he brought me to a shameful display of pleasure I was helpless to fight. *His*. Fallen from my perch on high to be his for the taking. To grant him immense power. To be made his eternal queen of this underworld of domination.

The firm muscles that defined his torso pressed against me, rattling my core. A vibration only a magical being could possess. And once this creature brought me to orgasm, we would be forever bound. He and I in a union so strong the tether between us would never be broken.

My moans peaked as he battled to decide which of my breasts he adored the most.

The left one. He worshiped it as though guzzling a life-sustaining nourishment.

I cried out from the pleasure he'd rained upon me. "Caleb. I'm..." I couldn't even finish the warning of my release. His mouth captured mine, stilling my will to say more.

His. Ruled over by him for eternity. As my orgasm hit, I could only pray for his shaft finally gaining a diamond-hardness to break through the ensnaring silver that ensured my purity.

"That was fucking amazing, Jules." He lowered me to stand on my own before he glanced outside. Even I felt the delight in having the best damned orgasm in my life in front of strangers.

That joy seemed too well lived as the small vibrator continued to jitter away against my core. "Caleb," I whimpered.

"Yeah. Of course." He reached down to the chastity device to shove a finger in, perhaps to push it to a better location. It only pressed more firmly to my nub with every attempt of his finger to capture it.

"Leave it right where it is." John's voice came from behind Caleb.

Fuck! We both panicked—Caleb fumbling and my breath halted.

The lighting above me came on like a weak spotlight, revealing our identities to the viewers outside. Slowly, John waltzed in, carrying a small silver box. "Caleb, get the tub so I can wash your slobber off my woman."

The vibrator may have brought me unimaginable joy, but it rapidly spiraled into misery. And worsened by the terror and excitement of John's tall form moving closer. But he was a tormentor. The cruel male come to destroy my happily ever after with Caleb.

"I'm not your woman," I spat, jerking against the bindings that trapped my wrists high.

"Yes, you are. And If you wanted pleasure this badly, you only needed to tell me." John's cruel words were accompanied by a contemptuous grin that quickly flattened, most likely hiding fangs that had sprouted. Now his scowl revealed his genuine emotions.

The cruel overlord's return guaranteed mine and Caleb's misery. All my sweet beta wanted was to ease my torment. We would both suffer; me, at the moment, enduring a continued rattle to my core that hummed loudly.

Caleb returned with a short black bucket, slow so as not to spill out the water.

"Go wait outside and enjoy the show." John's order had Caleb retreating from the bus. John kneed my legs apart and scooted the tub between them.

I forced the words out. "You're a terrible brother to him."

He knelt and lifted a wet rag from the basin, squeezing out excess water before rising. Everything he did happened slowly, as though he relished dragging out this torment.

"I spoiled him a bit too much, but that's what happens when we raise children that aren't ours." He ran the wet cloth along my lips.

I wasn't certain whether that was a jab at my upbringing. My teeth grit at the insult.

"I'm willing to share, so you're both happy." The alpha's body pressed to mine, forcing the vibrator against my nub and causing a hiss. "You're happy, right?" he asked, rubbing the cloth along my neck.

Rapid shakes of my head answered his question. I wasn't happy. It was absurd to believe this was conducive to happiness.

"Whyever aren't you happy, little Julie? You've even gotten the orgasm I've been denying you."

"Take it out!" I demanded, quivering as the sensation became too great. What the fuck was wrong with this delusional alphahole? He would spend my lifetime treating me this way.

"And what will you do for me?" he asked, dipping down for more water before raising it up to my chest. He pulled the sheer fabric above my breasts and squeezed the rag, permitting the warm water to roll down my breasts.

"Whatever you want!" My teeth chattered as he pressed more firmly against me.

"I want you laid out and begging me to pleasure you." He spoke like a sultan who'd found the least interested woman in his harem and placed a cruel demand upon her. "I want you thinking about me as you do it instead of getting all starry-eyed."

The rattling became too much for me to handle. Why did he demand so much of me? They were fantasies incorporated into my life. Why did it matter if my imagination made me happy?

"I will." I spoke quickly to end the orgasmic torment, wiggling as he moved backward while he continued to wipe my chest.

Classical music began to play. Romantic and slow cello. This had to be Caleb's effort to calm the beast.

There had to be plenty of good about John for my kind beta to choose to be around him. Something beyond John's willingness to raise his younger brother. I knew the hardship of the lives of people who had to raise children that weren't their own. They did spoil, and there was nothing wrong with that.

"John...please." I breathed, looking into the forest-filled eyes of mystery. Maybe, just maybe, he could open himself to reason. He had the power to end this ever-increasing discomfort. Maybe I could be the one to bring him to a change of heart.

"I'll be with you." I could force myself not to think and fantasize in order to end the punishments.

Private Performance

John assessed me, dragging out an eternal few seconds of my discomfort with the vibration before I finally felt the movement of the chastity belt as he unlocked it. It fell free, landing in the water and splashing the suds onto my lower legs. As did the vibrator fall and roll somewhere, the buzz rolling too far and silenced by the classical piece that played.

I shivered in appreciation at the freedom from the device that had turned to a horror. Now I knew the truth of the forced orgasms by a vibrator. The punishment that truly proved to be an agitating punishment. And I also knew the way it felt to have someone so caringly alleviate me of the discomfort that I'd deserved.

A gorgeous man who stepped closer and kissed me with passion. Kisses so much different from Caleb's. John's kisses held slow and methodical depth. They felt inspired by more than enrapturing heat. They matched the music from the speakers, which was slow and maybe disheartened. Much like a love story that drew out with uncertainty. The strings slowly wailed their need for something outside their grasp. Something elusive.

The pads of his fingers dug into the softness at my waist. Did he enjoy what he felt? Not the smoothness of a scrawny woman designed for a man of wealth. I was softer, lacking what made those women so perfect. Yet his tongue sought mine, no different than the cello pled for whatever it happened to be missing.

And what could this man be missing aside from the money spent to own me? What could he want? Me? Be that the case, what made me something of interest? A woman who'd posted silly pictures and short videos on the internet to draw attention to my grandmother's business? Sometimes themed to books in order to show my skills and bringing romance to life.

Be it regency or fantasy, dark or sweet, there could be a floral spread to any love that a person desired to experience. Maybe that drew him to me. Maybe the spread for a captive of a billionaire lover—

His hand fisted the hair at my nape. The beat had grown more playful, a piano now entering the scene. Had the missing piece been found? Whatever the cello so longed for. Did it rile this lover of mine who was desperate for a partner he could connect with? A torment of love. Or were we like Romeo and Juliet—

"Is this not entertaining enough for you?" he growled, scowling down to my hungry expression.

I swallowed. Of course it was. I paid attention to the experience. I even enjoyed the passion. "I…"

"You were thinking of something else."

I bit my lip, fearful of what might happen if my bulky captor grew angry. *Cello.* "I want you to play this number for me."

His eyes narrowed. Doubtful of my claim, perhaps.

"I know you have one. I saw it in your room." I waited, hoping for a sign he believed me. More words sped out of my mouth. "And I know the way you shift and move. You were the one who played at the masquerade, and it called to me." It wasn't a lie. He was a passionate man, and I couldn't help my wistfulness that took hold when he made music.

A ponderous expression overtook his features. The request was a good save. My fast thinking calmed the alphahole billionaire who'd researched and purchased me. The man who wanted me to be his wife to dote affections to him, even if he had to share me with his beta brother.

His responding flash of a sideways grin worried me, though. It didn't quite reach his eyes. "Of course, my darling love. Is music what you desire?"

Had I read part of that line once? Were they words a noble lover spoke to his damsel? Or perhaps a cruel prince. I didn't have time to ponder on the matter. I knew not to let my thoughts stray from John.

"Your music," I said in response to his offer, though hesitantly. This seemed far too easy. Like those moments in a book when I wanted to yell into a pillow to tell the heroine how obviously something about a man's behavior wasn't right. How falling for the trap was so stupid.

And weren't those obvious traps so much fun to dream about? The naivety of the protagonist or even outright lack of self-preservation. A foolish and oblivious act that anyone with half a brain knew not to fall for. Oh, the tension this man created deep in my psyche.

And, as usual, when John sucked me in as his prey, only one thing came from my hungry mouth. "Okay."

What had I okayed? In all the time I knew him, had I ever even told this alpha male no? The only thing to explain my loss of reasoning was how his musical abilities grounded me. The danger and darkness that lured me to say *okay* were usually preceded by his hypnotic abilities to awaken my soul with the cello. As though possessed, my mind pulled me thousands of directions, but always came back to him.

I most likely looked odd to anyone outside, already feeling drugged by the possibility of him performing for me. My drunken state as I stood under a light, still bound with hands close to the ceiling. Of course, the sheer outfit cast a magical or royal image of me as a captive awaiting my reward as John passed me in order to retrieve his beloved instrument. The one thing that might also calm the beast clawing within him, more-so than any act of sadism.

The music on the speakers stopped. Too dreadfully long, he made me wait before returning with a stand and cello.

Placing them to the side, he pulled out the arm of the couch, revealing the bench he'd had me bound on. Instead of setting it up for me, he used it as a seat and brought the cello to stand between his spread legs.

His entrancing stare held mine, as though he were a wizard about to cast a spell.

Even more exciting...no, not exciting, terrifying. Definitely horribly terrifying me of what was to come as he lifted his long wand into view. Would he cast a spell that left me forever incapacitated? I wouldn't let myself succumb, though.

I caught myself, lost once again to the magic he didn't tolerate. Also anxiously awaiting the grounding sounds only he had the perfected talents to create.

He adjusted his shoulders. The sexy adjustment I'd only ever seen a cellist capable of. His left hand found their mark, already pressing a few to a middle string as the bow slid like the heavens blessed it, creating a magnificent hum.

I'd expected a song that told of my blissful demise, because even that I loved. It only took a few seconds for me to know the music I'd so often heard at weddings. *A Thousand Years*. A passionately romantic song. One that had his eyes closed as the bow and his long, skilled fingers performed on the strings.

Visceral, that was how my being responded to this man whose redeeming quality poured out in tones. He became consumed with passion, and it showed when his eyes opened to take in the sight of me.

I must have appeared entranced by the song by the way he watched me. Perhaps he knew my heart beckoned to him, loving every moment of captivity as he worked his magic upon those strings.

If anything could bring me to him, it would most certainly be his love of music. His dedication to the art. His caring side that had brought him to spoil his younger brother, which proved a capacity for love.

I had tears in my eyes when the emotional number ended. Most anyone with a soul would be brought to such a state.

Carefully, he reached sideways and placed the cello on its stand, also placing his bow safely. I didn't want it to end. Not because of the sadist who was sure to return, but because of the way his music brought my world to perfection. Even those forest green eyes became the garden that would sustain me.

"Another," I said. "Just one more."

He huffed, smiling the terrifying smile. "Not yet. I've come bearing the gifts you've earned."

The romantic within him passed, as though the mask of humanity slipped away. The beast again took hold, overpowering the lovable part of him.

"Please, Sir," I said, fearful as he prowled my way. "Canon in D." That would surely calm whatever evil clawed to the surface.

"You should know by now..." he said, reaching up to my cuffed wrists. "I know you don't want for me to allow you to sweet talk or beg your way out of your punishment."

But that wasn't true at all. Experience of the mind was all I wanted. It was all I needed. Even the music didn't involve pain, only evoked emotion that I could grasp and control.

And yet this closeness, brought by the same eyes that entrapped me earlier, still brought me to want what I knew I shouldn't. He weakened my resolve, but it would return with full force. I wouldn't let myself become lost.

Adornment

Threat of upcoming pain or not, euphoria swirled within me. I still felt mostly overcome by the peaceful coaxing of the music that continued to reverberate in the depths of my lonely soul. For a few minutes, this man had completed me. At least his luring song accomplished such a feat.

But what would come, both now and for the rest of my life, was nothing to savor. Cruel pain, both to body and heart. A loss of freedom and control. Uncertainty no different from now, as my cuffed wrists were released. I lowered my arms, but this unshackling wasn't freedom by any means. He had something more to penalize me with. Now I preferred the security of the pole, and for him to go backward a safe distance from me.

With far too much grace, he did step away, but to the leather bench and guided it to its spot between the two poles. "On your back," he ordered.

What choice did I have but to obey? First, of course, I cast a wary glance at the couch. For the least I knew, he would lift the seat and retrieve a flogger from his arsenal of cruel devices that he'd neatly organized specifically for use on me.

If only I'd requested flowers as well when I asked him to play his cello. That would've helped with this endeavor. The blooms would've added a calming effect to charm the creature tormented and trapped in him that wished to devour me.

I lowered onto the bench and rested my back against the cool surface. Catching his hypnotic gaze. I still wanted to be immersed in them. I needed to seal my legs, but they widened in welcoming of him.

"This, my love, might hurt a bit." What he retrieved was small, sized no larger than a shoe-box for a toddler's feet, though more narrow. He removed a small square wrapper that held a first aid alcohol strip.

He needed to disinfect something for whatever might hurt? That sobering warning proved the sadist's return.

This never went well in novels. I started to scramble away, only for him to latch onto me at the waist as I attempted to twist off the cushioned bench.

He straddled me with ease. Taking my left arm, he secured the cuff of my wrist to the pole on my left side. He did so with the right wrist as well.

"I'll punish you for that insubordination next," he warned as he lifted himself off my immobilized body. By that point, his bulge had definitely grown. Not that he planned to use it for anything beyond pleasuring himself after a session torturing me.

"Please." My worry halted my ability to struggle. Just obey. I could still escape this torment if I submitted to his desire to rule my will. "I'll never—"

He raised a finger to his pursed lips before I could tell him I would never attempt to run ever again. Granted, I never read a dark romance where the promise not to run from a sadist held true. Those attempted escapes in novels were unbelievable anyway.

This man didn't seem to be the sort to let me go. Even the escape at the airport had been permitted or, rather, planned by him. And now, it wasn't as though the see-through slave outfit would help me fit into a crowd, even if I could get away.

He bent sideways to the pack and retrieved another disinfecting wipe. Once he took the wipe from the packaging, he shoved the sheer material upward from where it crisscrossed my breasts.

Now that I lay exposed under the spotlight, watchers could clearly see the one breast he rubbed the chill alcohol over. He meticulously sanitized the other nipple area as well, drawing out the time.

Sadist soulless monster.

Like a greedy vampire, this dark lord planned to draw blood.

He lifted some sort of medical scissors and placed the cold device on my lower ribs. Then, to my darkest dread of the evils of his sub-humanity, came the sight of the needle as long as a finger—and not near as thin as the ones on syringes. No one would subject themselves to that. Maybe if drugs or an excessive amount of alcohol were involved.

I couldn't stop the swells of my chest. Not even as he grabbed my left breast. I struggled to get my words out. "I–I promise–I–please, *Sir. Please.*"

His responding smirk flashed no teeth, but it did reach his eyes. That could mean any number of things. I didn't have to imagine an antihero from a dark romance; I had a real-life monster, just without the safety of written words.

"Right now, I only plan for these two piercings, but every offense will have this needle exploring lower. Starting with any further plea to stop me."

I bit my lips to hinder any response, squeezing my eyes shut.

"I know your fantasy about this."

He was wrong. I would never fantasize about this. Well, maybe once, but so much passion occurred in the one smutty scene that made it so sensual. The visual of the thin sparkling chains that dangled between, as though they were their own lingerie. The sensations felt every time fingers barely stroked them. Like they were being strummed. John could probably strum most magnificently.

"Your chest is quivering with excitement, Julie." He spoke so melodiously. The way he always said my name was far more beautiful than how anyone else ever said it.

I couldn't possibly be excited beyond the way it would feel in my mind. This was simply my imagination, my memory of something perfectly hot.

"You wanted punishment the night we met," he reminded me. "There are so many other ways I can discipline you instead of this, but your breasts will be adorned before this trip is over."

This seemed like another trap. But maybe the drugging effects of the cello conquered him, and this wasn't a trick. I still felt the high of the music.

And now, I needed to know what he considered as adornment. Maybe something worthy of a goddess. Or a thin, sparkly chain he could strum. Maybe he wasn't a sadist after all, just a man who planned to make me sparkle.

"Adornment?" I asked, then nibbled my lower lip to hide my interest in something that might accent my nudity in the most magnificent way, drawing attention to my breasts. It would also be better than a flogger. I could appear as a trapped siren the next time he played his cello for me. He could take in the sight of my entranced state brought about by his Faerie-born magical abilities, which would overpower my dark lure of him to his doom. That happened anyway whenever he played the instrument for me.

"You already decided what you want, but you won't even admit it to yourself," he said, firmly gripping my left breast. "And I doubt you consider this punishment."

Any discomfort caused by John would be punishment. Even if I enjoyed the result. But this would come, whether I stated my acceptance or didn't.

My hard bite to avoid the pain of his next action trapped my lips between my teeth. No words. No argument. Just look into those forested eyes and accept whatever he desired to do that I would both love and hate.

The horror of sharpness through skin registered. Were his eyes morphing to those of a monster, darkening and wickedly reflecting light? Would fangs form at the smell of my blood?

"Still your chest or this will hurt." His warning brought me to the realization of my panicked breathing and his strong hold of my breast and the prodding needle.

It felt as though the metal must have grown longer and thicker.

Dear God! Whyever had I been forsaken? What beautiful and pure angel such as I, unmarred by wickedness, would be tossed down from the heavens to be tormented in such a way by the evils of humanity? The evils of a beautiful, lust-worthy male who'd lured me to be his. To chain me by my breasts so I could never escape the dungeons created to house such a wiley being as myself.

He yanked up the scissor-like grabbers and pulled the torturous needle of ritual. All too quickly, he had them laid to my lower ribs again and another alcohol pad to where he'd just shoved something into me. Perhaps he was a doctor, but far from the hospital. This was simply a life-saving surgery after he happened upon me alone and in distress.

If only I had a penchant for medical romance. Maybe my broken, stockholm-syndromed mind would crave such literature after my escape from him. Though, I imagined it might annoy me to read the sanitization and ritual an author would include for those who needed to assess the true-to-protocolness and science of everything they read.

Did I fucking care enough to pay attention to that stupid unromantic detail meant for a medical training course? No, but the thought of it ruined this moment.

John was my shifter captor, that was all. He had magical healing saliva. But the one thing that would turn him into a fuck-hungry were-beast was blood. The overly stimulated nub between my legs awoke once again? This was my flesh pierced, and yet my body hummed in response to the wicked creature that performed the ritual.

Now he wiggled the spot where he'd pierced me. "Only one more to go. Contingent upon good behavior, of course," he said, again grabbing for the needle. I would most certainly pass out if I cared to see my breast that he now squeezed and the piercing needle angled for the next attack.

This time I whimpered, pulling helplessly at the poles my wrists were bound to. The next jab thrust in more swiftly than the last. But there was also something more. The ache at my center magnified, and an additional energy made this captor the only thing I desired awareness of. I craved his dominance more than I would ever have believed possible.

"Now then," he reached down to the box and pulled out the thin, sparkly chains that would connect to my new piercings and dangle. They were at least three connected to the clasps to swoop downward at different lengths to be admired. "I want to see these on you."

As he leaned close and connected the lightweight adornments to the new piercings, his touch and lustful gaze brought me to bonelessness to melt into the bench. The throb he attended to held not an ounce of discomfort compared to the ache he stirred between my legs.

"You liked that, didn't you, Julie?" His voice pulled me from my euphoric dizziness, as did his exploration of my folds. "You fucking loved it."

But I couldn't love it. Not me, the pure and good angel he'd unjustly captured. The one forsaken by the higher power that I served with the utmost loyalty.

Why were his damned eyes so mesmerizing? Like a forest I wanted to be chased through. To be captured and bound and mercilessly ravished in. And those broad shoulders that looked so beautiful whenever he held the bow.

He yanked the front of his pants down and plunged his swollen cock into me. "Oh fuck, Julie." He pumped all the way into me. "I never knew letting people watch me fuck could be such a turn-on."

This merciless beast...this warlord...no, this ancient and feral vampire would torment me into an orgasm. He probably thought of me as nothing more than a toy to torment—no different than a feline shifter playing with his prey.

"Look at me, Julie!" His demand forced me out of mind and to the thrusts that had my muscles straining, yet failing to aid me to break free of the bondage.

Every pump of his hips squelched with the overabundance of excitement he'd stirred inside me.

Even fiction never brought about this sensation. This...this connectedness to body and life. This attunement to my being. To another person. To that person's absolute bliss as he released himself inside me and stilled, breathing heavily. "That felt so fucking good, Julie. Too bad I have to punish you for your little act of defiance with Caleb."

But he couldn't get me so close to such an orgasm and stop. I'd loved what he did to me after his return. Even the piercing I would endure again to experience his passion.

"Please," I begged.

John didn't answer my plea. Instead, he let me *enjoy the outside view*, so any passerby had a view of me, and they all stopped for a good, long look. The sparkly chains swooping between the piercings didn't make me appear as the goddess I'd imagined they would. And the cord restraining my ankle made me more akin to a shamed slave on display. That went on into the next morning before the walls of the large vehicle hid me away and the journey began again.

Superbloom

Remaining with John or the close quarters outside his room made chances of private encounters with Caleb near impossible. And the limited routes and detours to reach the destination kept John in a foul mood.

Sure, he still enjoyed a firm hand, but he always brought me just shy of orgasms, so I became desperate for release. But, most punishing, he played his cello alone in his spacious room, letting only a trickle of sound escape for me to hear.

But right now, Caleb managed to sneak a visit to keep my spirits up. As always, the sight of him caused magical bliss to stir within me. And, oh, did I love the way he looked at my bare form as I waited on one side while bracing on one elbow with my palm cupping my cheek. A princess captured and awaiting salvation from the barbarian tyrant who ruled this lair of debauchery.

This caring beta that I adored looked absolutely gorgeous with his silky black locks freely flowing down to his shoulders. Like those werewolves who were too delicious to fear and could easily lure any woman they desired.

I perked up, raising onto a hip as he neared, gracing him with my posture of a goddess. Also loving the mischievous twinkle in his eyes that guaranteed my punishment to come if John discovered us. But the sting to my backside would be worth every moment in this hero's company.

Caleb spied past me to where the music escaped John's room. Once Caleb deemed the situation safe, his swagger had a sinful heat bubble within me. "I hear there's a super bloom ahead."

And that brought a bit of excitement to the detours we took. Today led us to an area I would absolutely love—if John let me see it. But his love of blooms would bring out his joy as well.

"You know what else?" my handsome beta asked, beaming wolfishly.

I shook my head with a starry-eyed loss for words. It was an act of mine that this charming lover proved to adore.

"Your knight in shining armor found the extra key John had hidden away." He lifted it to dangle from his index finger at eye level.

Now I was the one biting my lip in flirtation. I reached up to snatch it, but he pulled it away.

"Not until John takes his outing to get something special." He didn't say what the something special happened to be, but I knew it had to be something to do with more ways to punish me.

The music of the unknown piece John played slowed, and the hum of the instrument lowered.

We only had a minute at most if John decided to come out and torment me.

Caleb tucked the key into his pocket, whispering, "John's going to let us stop where you can look out on the flowers and I'll pick some as decorations."

This sweet beta proved to be so thoughtful, like one of those hard-working cowboys who innately knew how to treat a lady properly. Or the heroine's new best friend to carry her through the darkest times in an *enemies to lovers* romance.

"Soon." Caleb winked and raised, quickly turning and speeding through the sliding door to the front of the bus.

"Soon," I whispered to the empty silence.

I lowered to my side in my captive princess pose, knowing a mildly calm John might come out of the room at any moment. The hours spent earlier waiting for him to come out to me left me sore.

And I waited more, occasionally smoothing my hair if I tilted my head. And that movement usually caused the glittery jewelry chains that dipped between my breasts to angle oddly. I may have been captive, but I intended to be irresistible while fighting against such an evil wizard as him.

A while longer, and the touring bus stopped. Even then, my villainous overlord didn't immediately enter the space I'd become confined to. I always loved such a wait in books, but when true minutes ticked by and bare skin felt the chill of room temperature air, agitation and anxiety took hold of me.

The bus moved again and, after more time, the door finally crept open in my periphery, and my feigned indifference alluded to a lack of interest in the shirtless man who haughtily approached.

"That chain is plenty long for you to come to sleep with me," he said.

Not that I would ever admit to such a desire. "I'm rather fond of the floor."

"Then I'll open the walls so anyone with curiosity can see you."

That wouldn't do at all. Why would he even expect for me to give in and succumb to a need to go to him?

"Come to bed, Julie." Forced patience oozed from his tone. He had, after all, wanted an easy wife and a happy family. Coming to his bed must have been what he'd played music and waited for.

But he'd done things to punish me. He forced them upon me, shattering the fantasies I wanted to experience, and replacing them with discomfort. In his company, there were no beasts that hunted me. No warlord captured me. I could imagine nothing. He forced absolute acknowledgment and physical awareness.

I lifted my ankle, submitting to his expectation.

He accepted my agreement and lowered onto his knees, eyeing my adorned breasts as he lifted my foot to his chest.

I awaited the moment he might raise it to his shoulder and kiss his way up my leg and inner thigh. Or he could refuse to tolerate my insubordination and pull me upward by hips to meet his currently enraged cock, swollen in his smooth pants and ready for action.

By the way his attention remained on my form as he reached into his pocket, I couldn't rule out the possibility that the beastly desire to rule over me might be clawing at his psyche. But the key he retrieved proved other plans that involved a bed and a connectedness to this constant reality that I didn't care for.

Literary Ignorance

The key turned in the lock of the cuff, freeing my ankle.

I could push him away with the heel of my foot and attempt my daring escape—which was sure to fail. That would have me dragged into his bedroom to receive a punishment that I would have loved to read about from my cozy couch at home, but not something I cared to physically experience.

He stood and extended his hand downward to me.

Choosing a comfortable bed over punishment or sleep on the floor, I reached for his hand and let him pull me upright.

Once we were in his room, he ordered, "Leash yourself." He speedily shut and moved his white laptop from the corner of the made bed.

I crawled onto the smooth purple sheets, which did bring their own joy to the moment, even if they were nothing more than a captor's efforts to deceive me into enjoying the surroundings. At the headboard, a new glittery cord of silver awaited me. This one was longer than what he used on me during other occasions I slept in his bed.

I knelt on my knees in front of it and snapped the end in place, squeezing the padlock closed. My willingness to entrap myself for this powerful creature put me at his mercy. But I wouldn't dare look backward toward the undefeatable beast about to ravish his prize. Not even when I felt the dip of his weight on the bed that warned of his prowl toward me.

His palm lightly landed on my shoulder, roving forward to my sternum and applying enough force to pull me upright against his bare chest. His smooth face tickled along the left side of my neck, his lips catching on skin as they explored upward.

No heroine could deny her want for her antihero at this moment. Not a single one, aside from a truly boring book to be snapped shut. This man was no antihero, though, and I was no heroine, making my foolish joy of this touch all the more taboo. This would be one of those disappointing moments that reality forced upon a woman.

"Stop pretending you don't like me, Julie." The lightness of his mouth as it traced my left jawline sought weakness in my resolve. But I had to deny him all the more.

He was just a man—a boring, albeit competent at claiming me, man. Also gorgeous, for a regular man. But I could see the dragon readying to shatter my defensive walls.

That refusal of mine brought his hand from my sternum to my right cheek, guiding my head to turn toward his. Directing me to enchanting eyes that had mastered trickery and wicked magic.

Damn him and his dark powers! He'd heated me to the core of my soul. Magnificently so. The sort of bubbly hotness that made me thankful this chastity belt didn't permit him to explore the part of me that ached to be touched.

His lips connected to mine. Warm and consuming. As magnificent as those happy endings. The ones where every conflict had been resolved before the happily ever after arrived in all its vibrant, heart wrenching glory. Where the shy beauty kissed him in return because he finally earned her affection.

The pads of fingers, both gentle and forceful—but bearing no beastly claws—explored my body.

Forget that happy ending kiss I initially believed it to be. This was the moment of passion. The fiery connection to root for that would set the stage of the attraction that would continue to blossom.

Even the way his roaming hands bumped my breasts or momentarily tugged at the weightless, shimmery chains that dipped from the piercings sent a greater flare through me. Like an enchanting Egyptian queen and her powerful lover, both of whom were drunk upon the lust for each other.

My crown, weighted with sovereign jewels, crashed down. As did the chastity belt once cruelly placed upon me. Their shattering freed me of the once infallible oppressor.

My hero's triumphant kiss was accompanied by him lowering me onto my right side as he too followed, tilting me onto my back in a field of magnificent blooms of purples and beiges splashed with pinks and blues. And when he had me laid out for his pleasure, his strong frame shielded me from any dangers—not that he'd allowed any to remain.

Anticipation mounted with time compounding upon itself as I awaited his body to lower and connect with mine. That he would consummate our binding. On this holy matrimonial bed of the silken petals of my most cherished flowers. It was the way any woman would crave for her innocence to be lost.

I awaited it. That plunge into me that would forever join us. The moment of his mastery over me as I submitted to his power. The pumps that would ignite me with an eternal flame for him alone.

...and I continued to wait, longing for the moment he so cruelly teased me with.

...and I waited some more.

A manly sigh preceded my lover moving backward.

And, just like a sleeping princess who'd awoken after a hundred-year rest, my eyes fluttered open.

He rose from the bed, strong back muscles shadowed, before he picked up a white tee shirt and pulled it on.

I sat upright. "John?" I hadn't done anything wrong. I'd been enjoying his touch. More than simply enjoying it, I loved it. Well, aside from a few visions of him as a magnificent hero. But what was wrong with that? They were thoughts of him.

I scooted to the edge of the bed until the leash stopped me. "Don't leave."

He turned, with one brow already raised in sarcasm. "I'll send for your fantasy wonderland boyfriend."

He was mad at me? And after the miserable hours I'd spent waiting for him to come to me earlier? I had the right to be angry about this. And, ready to rise from the ashes, I didn't fear repercussions.

"No," I snapped, crossing my arms, which awoke my recently pierced nipples. I attempted to readjust, but he'd already seen my awkward movement.

"You don't want to play rugged cave princess with Caleb?" he asked, leaning his back against the wall.

I was fond of those ice caves and the battles for captive females. The conquer and the bindings I couldn't break free of as I became the spoils of war.

"Ice Cave Sovereigns." Okay, maybe that book was a bit extreme in its caveman time-period themes. And the cover was a bit cheesy with the Sabre-riding cave warrior royals with spears. "It was a good book."

"I'm sure it was," he muttered, readjusting his erection in his pants. It wasn't like he'd lost interest in sex. He just wanted to frustrate me.

"Read it if you don't believe me." I moved backward on the bed to ease the tension on the sparkly leash, kneeling in my wait for him to return.

"It's unrealistic."

"Unrealistic?" I spat the word back to him. I raised my hands to the surroundings in frustration. "And a decked out touring bus with a dungeon is realistic? This is the fantasy of a boy who kept his head in the comic books with busty females because he didn't know how to talk to a real girl."

Mentioning his lack of skill with women may not have been my wisest moment, given his indignant scowl. But that was a kind of cute expression, especially with his tousled hair.

"I never read comics!" he spat, breathing in a way I expected flames at any moment. "Or any other brainless garbage."

So, he considered the books I read as brainless garbage. Funny, given how he enjoyed my hobby of floral arrangements inspired by novels.

"I'll have you know, some of what you call garbage deals with the complexities of being a human." I stuck my nose up defiantly. I would win this argument, just as I had plenty of times with other judgmental people. "You could make fast pals with a few of the judgmental locals given your literary ignorance."

It began to feel like that *enemies to lovers* moment. The ones that had my heart racing for more action from the stubborn couple. At least, until John hastily turned to the door and yanked the handle.

But he couldn't leave. I wouldn't let him. "John!" I went as close to the edge as I could, reaching outward in the direction of the slamming door.

And therein proved why fiction would always be more engaging than a man who chose to leave a situation than deal with his issues. Or any interactions that brought about these emotions that so many people hated to deal with but refused to escape.

Little Red

It didn't take but about twenty minutes before the bus came to a stop. For an hour or so, I bubbled with anger at John's nerve to call one of my favorite pastimes garbage. I'd been an idiot to feel some fictitious desire blossoming between us.

He'd been a kidnapper, controlling my life. He'd bound me and rained down punishment. And no matter what, I would never admit to him I'd begun to enjoy that part of this experience. But he insulted my most beloved hobby, just as other people had throughout my life. I felt as though I'd endured a debate at a backwoods rally and the losing opposition proudly walked away with the certainty that departing determined their victory.

All too soon, the door clicked. I wasn't ready to see John, and I wouldn't submit to any punishment.

I didn't bother looking toward the entry. I wouldn't acknowledge John ever again within this lifetime. At least, not until he apologized for everything he'd said to deliberately insult me.

"Jules," came the familiar and affectionate call from Caleb.

I should have been just as angry at him. He'd helped set my capture in motion. He wanted me for his own delights.

"You're mad too?" He came to stand at the foot of the bed with a picnic basket in tow.

That morsel of information caught my attention. John must have said something to Caleb about his escape from confrontation.

I sat up, clutching the smooth sheet that wrapped me. "Why would anyone be mad?" I asked, keeping an air of calm while glancing at the basket, which must have had fun goodies or another piece of delightful clothing.

"John seemed absolutely livid when he stormed off." Caleb knelt on the bed and crawled my way, still holding the basket. "He even had food packed for a secret romantic excursion. But he told me to take you out instead."

Now came that moment of awareness. I should have simply refused to care for any kindness. No matter how I wanted to respond, my earlier insults to John might have been too harsh. Men didn't bother with romantic gestures. At least, not in real life. Though, Caleb's charm was a rare, true jewel amongst men outside of books. And now, possibly, John did something kind for me.

"John wanted to do something nice for me?" I asked, my stomach rapidly sinking with the weight of self-inflicted nausea at the acknowledgment. I didn't really think John was bad with women. He played beautiful music, bringing me to a grounding place I loved.

"Only an idiot wouldn't do wonderful things for you." Caleb leaned forward with a small key and worked it into the little padlock.

Peeking from the basket, I saw the thick purple spine of a book. Now I didn't know if John was some wounded antihero. Someone who wanted to be good but needed to outgrow his flaws.

He's the villain. He kidnapped and punished and pierced me! I can't ignore that barbaric behavior.

I tightened the sheet at my chest before lifting the book, *A Complete Guide to Wildflowers.*

"Jules." Caleb freed the leash from my collar.

I was in the right. John overreacted! He'd gotten me steamy and bothered before randomly getting angry while I experienced him in a sea of blooms.

"Jules?"

I had every right to call out John's ignorance about my preferences.

But he'd been so nice. We'd shared true love's kiss that was sure to lead somewhere amazing. Our bodies were on fire for each other—

I'd insulted him.

But he insulted me first!

"Julie." Caleb said my name softly, similar to the sound of John's voice.

I let the book slide down into the basket as I met Caleb's worried stare.

"Are you okay?" he asked.

"I am."

"John mentioned clothes for you to put on. But maybe we should do something fun first." Caleb lovingly teased the sheet downward, tugging it against my sensitive peaks. At my hiss, he let go of the sheet as it dropped to expose my beautifully adorned breasts.

"Sorry. I'll let those heal before doing all the things I want to do." He looked around the room to a narrow set of drawers on the other side of the bed.

At least he proved not to enjoy causing me pain.

While Caleb went to the drawers, I looked into the picnic basket that didn't fully close. There was a bottle of wine poking from beneath the blue blanket, and a pack of cut strawberries and chocolates. Probably another pack of food below that.

"Red or black?" Caleb asked, startling me from my examination of the items. I glanced over my shoulder to his charming smile. God, was he one of the sexiest men alive, and overflowing with sweetness.

My head whirled with the many emotions of the day. "Whichever," I replied.

His fiendish grin with pearly teeth almost looked as though a fang captured part of his lower lip. "How about you be my Little Red?"

My heart skipped beats in my chest at the thought. *Abso-fuck-ing-lutely.* He knew how to set me alight.

But no matter the way I felt about Caleb, John was the dark fantasy come to fruition. I couldn't; I wouldn't physically endure what I loved to read. I needed to get away before the guilt of my quarrel with my captor returned to make me foolishly believe John was a compassionate man. I had no choice but to do it while Caleb took me out to play as his Little Red.

A Picnic

The thick folded clothing Caleb laid out beside me turned out to be a vibrant crimson corset with lacy off-shoulder sleeves and a silk skirt overlaid with black lace and ruffled that came to mid-thigh at most. It was beautiful. The sort of beautiful that women stopped and stared at when passing a display mannequin.

"John got me this?" I asked, surprised. Beneath, there were even a pair of cute black ballerina style flats.

Another pang at how I'd treated John struck me. But no dress would ever prove him to be charming. That beautiful rose of a man had far too many thorns.

"Course he did, Jules. Looks like I'm under-dressed for this picnic, though." Caleb still looked absolutely spectacular in his indigo jeans. "I'll change while you get ready." He pecked my cheek and quickly left with the basket in tow.

The moment he disappeared from sight, I rushed to put the dress on. Which, given the top was an actual corset like from the Victorian era, became a bit difficult to manage, since I needed it tightened. Not to mention how much the pressure hurt my sore breasts.

Caleb returned in a black suit, swaggering over and eager to help me with the strings at the back of the garment.

"I need my wolf mask." He looked too gorgeous with his slight beard and only half of his hair in a topknot. It was a gorgeous style that few men could pull off. I didn't need him to wear a mask to make this trip outdoors perfect. Or, rather, this escape.

With the corset tightened, his palm smoothed over the silk at my front, then down to the ruffles, teasing me with his exploration and discovering that no panties accompanied the dress.

"Damn, Jules." He purred against the side of my neck. "I want to fuck you now *and* once we're outside rolling in the flowers."

Flowers. I'd wanted to see them earlier. Just the thought of laying on the silky petals and the fragrance as Caleb made love to me had me keen to his fingers that caressed my inner thigh. I wanted him to have me laid out—

No. I just needed to get away. I could fantasize about what I wanted him to do to me once safe and far away.

Caleb's lips trailed to my shoulder, adding more need between my legs, where his fingers successfully migrated to my bare core.

He hummed against my skin. "I need this, Jules."

My shallow breaths stopped. This I loved; the way he desired me and couldn't wait. But I couldn't waste time.

I flirtatiously pushed his hand from where I wanted it to be. "Only once you catch me."

Something between a whimper and a hum escaped him as I snatched the shoes and slid them on. But as I stepped toward the door, the sight of the cello caused me to hesitate. No one ever played so beautifully as John did. It was a part of him. His strumming, his broad shoulders. The way he grounded me to the reality of him I did truly love.

But it was nothing more than a heroine's doom to remain here with the two brothers.

Or was staying the right thing for her to do? Maybe in a novel, but I was no flawed heroine. Men always caused a suffering that only foolish people endured. I'd seen it repeatedly with friends and acquaintances. I'd arranged flowers for some of the same people for their second and third weddings after divorcing their supposed true love.

Resolved to escape, I continued onward. But passing the dungeonous area made me want to cringe and break things as well as remain and accept John's mastery—even have his child. To play with Caleb while also letting the elder brother's sadism come out.

Caleb swept past me with a basket in hand. "John has it set so you can't get out on your own. But he wants for you to get to go out before night sets in."

"Night?" I asked.

"It's already five-thirty, Little Red."

When we arrived at the semi-front area, he pressed buttons on the wall, which opened as a door. He quickly hopped out and turned to help me, but the late afternoon view of the super-bloom already enraptured me.

"Are you cold?" he asked.

I couldn't stop myself from being lost in the hilly carpet of colors of the wildflowers that stretched toward a tree-line not too far to my left. Pinks and purples—my favorite shade of purple—and blues and reds. All adorning the landscape. And beyond the hill was the peak of the roof of a white house, which made this look like one of those photos that made people giddy at the symbol of serenity.

No one, not even John, could deny the magnificence of this area. And I felt a bit saddened to know he'd been too angry to enjoy it. There were sides to him I liked. Especially the way he played the cello. And the way he could bring me to orgasm. He could probably do both at the same time out here.

"Jules?" Caleb said, drawing me to him.

I finally caught on to the words he'd spoken. "I'm not too cold." And in the low sixties, I would get hot running, anyway. Though, I would love a red cloak to top off the Little Red appearance.

"Good." My handsome shifter took my hand and led me out onto the blanket of colors.

I pointed to the nearby tree-line. "Can we go that way?"

"Absolutely, Little Red."

If only he knew I would run into those trees. That I would hide and escape both brothers. I'd go home and lock myself away and build a tall fence so they couldn't get to me.

I held to my wolf's powerful hand, occasionally side-eying him. Each time, he happened to also be side-eying me, but with a large, toothy grin.

"I know you plan on running," he mused, "and you know I'll capture you."

The corset seemed to tighten with my delighted inhale.

He could pin me to a tree, twisting my arm behind my back as he pumped into me. He could even have me on the ground bent over beneath the green canopy, spanking or claiming me. Maybe both.

"I hope so," I replied, unable to fight my responding glow. But I knew it wouldn't be Caleb to capture me. It would most likely be John, which gave me all the more reason to get as much distance as possible.

Down the hill as we walked, the two-story country home came into view. And there were lines of cars parked around it. Several vehicles that had parked and mashed the flowers. A large sign on the side of the house had bold letters. *The Assembly House.*

I glanced back to the massive bus, not spotting John. There would have been so few directions he could have gone. Just a few side road options, but he hadn't stopped here to go to that Assembly House. I may not have known him well, but I knew him well enough by now that he wouldn't go there.

"How about right here?" Caleb asked when we were around five or six yards from the forest, lowering the picnic basket. I had to agree that the spot was close enough to the trees that I could make my swift getaway.

Caleb shook out the small blanket. "You aren't even enjoying the flowers."

I brushed the curiosity of the escape from my mind and smiled at him. He was too busy to see me searching out options. At least he pretended to be too busy. "Just thinking," I replied.

He spread the blanket next to where the picnic basket waited for us to open it and dine.

"You're so perfect." Caleb's words made me feel absolutely beautiful. He'd always made me feel that way. He sat on the blanket and pulled items from the basket to in front of him to look through. He set the wildflower book out and slid it near my feet.

John had gotten that for me as a gift. It was a simple kindness that made me feel a painful tug at my heart that I had to shove out of my mind. I needed to leave the brothers while I had a chance. Nothing would change my mind.

Caleb toyed with the frills of the skirt, drawing my attention to the way he bit his lower lip with wolfish amusement. "There might be big, bad wolves in those woods."

I smiled downward to where he sat. "You're right here."

"Guess you're right." He stretched back to pillow the back of his head with his hands. "Want to see what big things I have?"

I definitely wanted to, but there wasn't time for a last moment of passion. Before I could come up with an excuse not to, a hardly audible drumming came from the forest. It was both intriguing and concerning; exciting while unnerving.

Caleb didn't seem to mind the beat from within the forest at all. "I believe I left something behind on the bus." He held a hand upward for me to help pull him up, which I did, and he used that hold to come even closer and lightly peck my lips. "Don't you go anywhere. We still need to have fun."

The next low beat that rang out felt like a timer had started. I feigned reluctance to part from Caleb, but he knew a chase would begin.

The Assembly

Were my life a book that I currently read, this moment would be when I furiously waited and hoped the heroine wouldn't leave. And, strangely, even now, I had my second guesses about my own choices. The handsome man, my big bad wolf, now several yards away, proved to be precisely what I wanted in life. A man who loved to play as much as me. Someone who brought the magic I could experience.

But then there was John. To have one brother required the other. Not a *why choose*, but a captive and her master with the nice brother to sneak visits.

I stood. This time I knew I had my chance at escape—and not just a pretend run and being caught. Freedom to return to my blissful world of books and fantasies. Of pleasure without the pain. Just the way I wanted my life to be. The fantasies I longed for would play out under my control—contentedly alone.

The thud of a beat, low and menacing, came again, though. Like the beat of the forest's heart. A fantastical world, perhaps? A hunt that was about to begin—

I needed to clear my mind of absurd wishes. I could return to this idea once home and safe.

With all the courage I could muster, I ran toward the forest. And as though it knew I requested entry, a stronger beat arose. One that made the rich sunset take on a new form as it called forth the evening. Perhaps a sacrifice or burning of witches would soon begin.

In my head were both Caleb and John. Everything a girl could want. Everything I wanted if they were characters inked upon the pages of a book. But real life didn't have perfect captors. And real life also didn't have a drumming coming from perfectly located trees, either.

Yet there was, in fact, a drumming that had nothing to do with my imagination. One which warned that something wasn't quite right about where I wanted to seek refuge.

With only one choice, I bolted through the colorful blooms and over the hill, then down toward the proud little *Assembly House* on the close hilltop. There I would find people to help me.

I looked back toward the bus, but Caleb wasn't within sight. He would have expected me to choose the forest. And if it were only him and me, I would have chosen the hunt. To be his Little Red.

Now I ran faster toward the building that granted me freedom from him. There would be people. Several people to help me. Or even let me borrow a phone so I could call Roy.

Just the thought of seeing him again slowed my steps. Sure, he'd been my go-to for company. He even helped people, so he would probably help me. But I could never settle for his company again. He might expect more from me if I attempted to contact him. It would be just me and my books and my flower shop. That was what I wanted. No one else.

I continued toward the doors of the white building that beamed with the glow of waning sunlight. It seemed to call me forth to it for protection. To where I would receive refuge behind intricately carved doors. To return to my life of old.

When I pushed those wooden doors open, there was a crowd of people seated in folding chairs facing away from me. But when the heavy doors slammed at my back, heads, many hidden beneath caps, turned to face me. Eyes of the people all peered, measuring me in my out-of-place corset dress. There must have been over a hundred people, mostly scruffy men.

I looked ahead to a standing man in faded jeans, who adjusted the cap atop his head and scowled in my direction.

Fuck!

This was the last thing I expected. Roy had attended a few of these gatherings before. He'd even invited me. But the one he'd dragged me to had only a dozen disgruntled people. And they weren't anything like what I saw now.

But I couldn't hesitate to get help, not when my freedom was at stake. Not when failure could end my chances at an ordinary life. I sought out a friendly face. A smile. Somebody who looked eager to help me as I walked further in. All the while, stares remained glued to me with piercing disdain.

My confidence in this route for escape began to waiver. Maybe the forest would have been better. But I'd grown up with absurd judgment and sneers all my life. Most people had a distaste in my willingness to be different, but they wouldn't shun someone in need of help.

"A heathen who partakes of the vile happenings within the forest is among us." The man at the front scoffed. The hand he extended to point a finger at me didn't waiver.

"One of them." The muttered words, which oozed with accusation, came from my right.

Them wasn't good to be associated with in this company. It was the sort of thing no one dared admit to. It gave the speaker the right to incite hostility. Even people who didn't fully agree would still obey for fear of being lumped in with a *them*.

I shook my head. "No. Not one of them. I just need a phone."

The debilitating silence from the *Assembly House* had me desperate to find anyone that remotely seemed caring. Several of the scruffy-looking people stood, squaring their shoulders in a way that suggested aggression.

One held a leather book to his chest. Books were friendly. Books inspired. But they weren't supposed to inspire weapons on a man's hips. Another man stood, an even larger weapon slung to his side.

This *was* one of those elusive extremist gatherings where everyone carried several weapons. The ones that were like their own self-proclaimed militias that took over towns that no one stopped at, since every local openly carried weapons they looked overly-eager to use. It was as bad as the books with mafia setups—minus the expensive suits and rationality.

Even a sheepish attempt at a smile didn't make me feel as though a compassionate connection would be possible. I just needed to back out of this place of hypocrisy and conspiracies.

Too many eyes followed me as I took my steps backward. I could still escape these nut jobs. Though movement from someone with a weapon seemed to match my every step.

There comes a point when playing it cool isn't as effective as a flat-out run. As I realized that the time for escape had come and was about to pass, I turned to run for the door.

But then I saw Roy near the door. He attended the rallies and small disgruntled gatherings, but never anything like this.

"Come begging for me to take ya back, you cheating harlot?" Roy spat. He didn't seem to be himself. Just cold and bitter. As though the worst influencers took him in during his time of despair.

My backward step landed against the hard leg of a chair, and the angry faces all around held a sort of delight at the sight of my terror.

"I want to go home." My trembling foot sought more distance from the man who'd assumed I would ever consider settling down with him. Maybe I should have years before the brothers arrived in my life. I could have accepted the miserable fate of nothing more out there for me. Doomed to unhappiness and tuning out the never-ending judgments and passive-aggressive comments because I was a *them*.

"Apologize and I might look past you being a slut!" Roy demanded.

I had nothing to apologize for. I'd committed no wrong against him. I could do whatever I wanted with my own body with whoever I wanted. And I wasn't a slut. But this wasn't a time to defend myself or argue. This was a time to leave.

"We were to get married, me and you, damn it! And you go fucking city boy, baby-eaters." Roy readjusted his cap, and I could see the wetness in his eyes.

Gasps and shocked sounds broke the long moment of apprehensive silence.

I could look nowhere that disappointment and disgust weren't oozing from someone. They didn't even know me. They only knew his delusional lies. And he'd latched on to their hypocritical hatred of true personal freedoms for everyone.

Maybe I was sorry for his hope in having me. He wasn't this hostile of a person before. At least, not toward me. "I never tried to lead you on, Roy. I've already told you that."

"They all know you wronged me; you darned lying snake!" He threw his hat onto the floor near his foot. "It's just how your kind are. All the same."

"Round here we teach our women to submit." From behind me, a man's voice seemed to reverberate in my skull. "Might take a heavy hand, but she'll make things right."

The fuck if I would! They could all go straight to hell!

Now I did feel the dilemma of the trapped heroine in need of action.

Roy marched my way, as though I was his to capture and cage as his wife in need of a heavy hand.

No. That would never be my fate. I'd rather be wandering about outside in the wilderness with bears and wolves than such a fate as this.

I bolted forward, knocking Roy off-balance as I rushed for the door. As I reached the handle of the door and pulled, someone behind me grabbed my forearm. But with the door already open and revealing the haunting dusk before me, I didn't dare risk being trapped. I pulled free of whoever attempted to capture me, racing from the building and straight for the silhouette of the forest. A backdrop of a fiery orange of the last trickles of day made the refuge seem ominous, but not so bad as what I'd just barely escaped.

Lost

The distant sound of a drum didn't hinder me as it had when I began my escape. I could run toward that sound and away from Roy's grating voice that pursued me. Onward toward what one man called *heathens of the forest*. To be called a heathen by a man like that meant whoever he spoke of wasn't anyone to fear. The ones doing the name calling and toting weapons to intimidate others were the sort to worry about.

Thankfully, the tree-line wasn't far, and no one from *the Assembly* deemed me worthy of capturing. When I arrived at the safety of the trees, out of breath and calves inflamed, brief flashes of light welcomed me into this mysterious world with a clear path of smooth dirt. I could only assume the flashes to be fairies, leading me to sanctuary in the forest's heart where the distant thud beckoned.

But wasn't that the sound as the hunt began? As the wolves were freed.

Caleb.

I spun, searching the dimness that didn't allow me too much vision beyond silhouettes. But further in, I could see the traces of golden light, which seemed like it must be from torches. The light of the heathens that welcomed me.

What if Caleb waited in the shadows along the path? He could easily pounce on me as I sought a place to hide and wait.

My every cautious step forward had my mind racing with all the ways Caleb might capture me. Whether it be him pinning me to a tree or tossing me onto the dirt path to ravish me. Both were possible. He could also drag me away with a hand covering my mouth as I furiously kicked to escape him. But he could easily have me laid out on a mossy boulder within seconds, binding me just as a Fae of this forest would do.

These thoughts got me into this mess with the brothers. I needed to think clearly and remember the life I once lived. The safety and security of my solitude.

I quickened my steps, closing in on where light trickled through a wall of thick foliage ahead. Where the slow drumming grew louder. And where I heard music begin, but not just any music. Strings. As though these *heathens* had a love for the arts. But nothing like John's skill.

I peered through the leaves into the torch-lit area that must have stretched for a while, spotting cheerful people and festival booths. Singles, groups of friends, and even doting couples were within sight. Some sneaking in or out of colorful little caravan wagons that looked like tiny homes of the traveling festival workers. All wore renaissance attire, and some even had floral crowns of freshly picked blooms. A few were in scarlet corset dresses similar to mine, though theirs were long and elegant. I could somewhat blend with the crowd.

But what if this was another one of John's games? What if he'd wanted me to think I could find an escape here? He'd done it before. And just as before, Caleb allowed it to happen under his watch.

At least this was still better than Roy and *the Assembly* cultists. But to take the steps out into the festivities meant exposing myself. If I waited in the woods, the most bright light to shine upon me would be the fireflies. That, I could conclude, would be the safest thing to do.

"Are you lost?" John's question hadn't even finished before I jolted, my heart racing as I spun to see him. But the minimal lighting didn't expose him. And while that did terrify me, it ignited a dip in my stomach.

The sudden onset of my panicked breath reminded me of just how tight this corset squeezed me.

"Or maybe—" he stepped into view from behind a tree "—reminders of home weren't as fun as you thought."

"John, I..." Why were words so difficult in his presence? Even Caleb, in all his wonder, didn't cause the reaction within me that John did. This man, though sadistic as he may have been, always sent my mind reeling. An antihero I would absolutely love the thoughts of, if not for the reality of him.

His slow saunter my way seemed to push all noise and activity from my senses. He spoke, "Stop pretending you don't want this, Julie."

I loved how my name rolled off his tongue. I had since the first time he said it.

The calm control in his timbre had my knees wobbling beneath me. It was nothing like the boring men like Roy. The ones I easily escaped the physical presence of by imagining something more in life—something magical in a faraway place.

In a way, I did want the gorgeous man who drew too close to me. But he was an unpredictable person who could do any number of things, be they pleasurous or painful. But torment was what he had planned for me. I could see it in the flare in his eyes; feel it in the steady swells of his chest. Even the set of his barely visible brow informed me I had no say in whatever came next.

I'd infuriated him earlier, cutting deep enough that his genuine resentment of my words caused him to storm out. And there would probably be unbearable consequences for that encounter.

My tall captor stepped in front of me. "You couldn't even spend five minutes surrounded by the unhappy reality that awaits you if you return home."

"I have my flower shop and home." I didn't have to be around anyone once I returned to my former life.

"You can have those things anywhere we go. And me doing to you the things you stay up late at night wishing for," he said.

Even the way he spoke made the threat so deceptively promising. I didn't want any fictional scenarios of romance to go beyond being words on a page.

"That's not what I want," I replied. I couldn't explain why to him, but it didn't matter.

His next step that had his body against mine gave me too few options for escape. At best, I could attempt to force my way backward through the foliage I stood against. It seemed to be nothing more than a weak barrier.

"It was *all* that you wanted on the night we met," he said.

I'd wanted the one-night stand. The feel of powerful hands on my body. A separation from him before the passion fizzled out. I wanted the encounter I could always look back upon and relive again and again, always tweaked to perfection.

The torchlight that trickled through to him added to the minacious expression. Raising a finger to my chin, he tipped my face upward. "We want each other."

I shook my head, breaking his hold on my chin. Only him in my fantasies, where all the disturbing bits and the mundane events could be removed. There was no happy ending with what he had planned. It would only be a loss of myself; acceptance of a life that I had no control over.

Knowing the dreadful future of succumbing to this growing physical attraction, I pushed his chest. Not that it budged, but I surprised him enough that I could force myself backward through the leaves of the narrow bush and spun to run into the crowds in the festival.

Reflections

I didn't dare turn backward to see if he pursued me while speedily weaving through the cheerful crowd. I didn't slow down either, not until I'd arrived at the larger structures where the torch lighting barely reached.

This area appeared to have carnival rides and booths. It was a stark contrast from the adult renaissance theme, leading me to wonder if this open area was an out of season fairground. I finally took the chance to scan my surroundings for John, whose height would stand out in the crowd in the lit area.

I saw no one I recognized, but John would be somewhere nearby. I needed a place to hide in order to escape from what the brothers would forever subject me to.

Determined to find an overnight refuge, I searched the dark area. The carousels cast in shadow were quite the unnerving sight. Combined with the empty booths, the place seemed more like a dystopian scene that would probably house horrors. Yet nothing looked excessively old or broken down as I snuck toward a tall metal structure.

By the size of the building, it must have been a place for staff during seasonal operations.

This building might pass as a hiding spot for the night. Given my last experience entering a building, I wasn't eager to go in, though. But staying out in the open meant giving up. It meant accepting whatever future John had planned for me.

Behind me, the slow drumming stopped, and a cello called out to me. Not just any piece, a calming one John had played before. Deceptive music. Music I easily longed to enjoy. To be pulled into a moment and memory of him at his finest.

If he thought that would call me to him, he was wrong. I looked back to the torch-lit area, already overcome by the way the music affected me. How could he easily draw me from my racing thoughts and into the moment where I enjoyed everything? There were so many bubbling emotions that only he'd ever been able to bring out.

Experiences I would get to spend a lifetime re-imagining and perfecting, so long as I got away. And what trap would I blindly fall into if I permitted such a call to lead me like a moth to a flame? To a night of humiliation and a life succumbing to his sadism. I had to get away from my billionaire captor who'd discovered my weakness.

With new certainty for escape, I turned to the tall metal building, more resolved than ever that I needed to get away. I rushed up the rickety metal stairs at the back of the building, patting at the wall for a door, which opened, and I snuck inside.

Deep Purple light awakened and greeted me, both from above and in a triangular pattern on the floor. Although I expected this to be an area where people could relax or get dressed, it turned out to be a hauntingly silent, unending place.

A mirror maze. The lighting looked as though it went on in-definitely, but that was the illusion of several perfectly angled mirrors—some of which cast reflections of me. Even searching the area above, I found no escape route to climb to. Only more small purple lights that offered aesthetic illumination.

Trying to hide from the brothers in here would end in capture, so I turned back. I only found a mirror with the outline of the wide door, but so similar to the cut of all the mirrors. I pushed my reflection, but the mirror didn't give way to the outside world.

This was no escape at all. This felt like an endless sight of me from every single angle. Looking at my reflection outlined by the purple made this feel as though the true antagonist finally caught up and stared back at me. Taunting and cruel. Mocking me for my terror.

But I wouldn't let that play of light and reflection scare me. I needed to figure out how to get to the front entry to escape this place. I turned to another endless sight of mirrors. Even the pattern of purple lights on the floor blended perfectly with the reality-bending reflections.

I extended my hand, prepared to pat my way out of here and to somewhere I could actually navigate. In a way, I felt doomed, seeing myself dressed in something so frilly and immodest. Aside from the vibrance of the purple illumination, I looked no different than the night I met the brothers. Except now a collar and cuffs adorned my wrists and ankles. In all likelihood, I could be walking into a trap where these cuffs would be put to use. Somewhere that I would be required to see countless reflections of my punishment to come.

That realization propelled me forward a few steps until my palm landed on a cold surface. The connection to a mirror was evidence enough that I could find a way to an exit. I wouldn't let this be the trap that doomed me. I wouldn't be forced to live the life anyone else had planned for me. I could go back to my world of flowers and books and be content.

Patting as I went, I cautiously continued my escape, feeling my way along the passage where reflections of me from various angles continued in an endless taunt. After around the tenth tall mirror, I felt a corner, then the next reflection of my disheveled self. This one wobbled with the pressure of my hand.

Finally, another mirror that acted as a door.

I gladly pushed it and stepped through. Lights flickered to life, brighter and of multiple colors and streaks across the floor. The illumination against mirrors only made this area look endless as well. Turning and attempting to return to the other hall met me with nothing but an unyielding reflection.

There could be any number of these one-way mirrors. They could send me in circles no differently than how John sent my mind reeling in all directions. I might become trapped.

Now I walked, paying attention to my reflections as I sought the true path to freedom. That only seemed to land me too close to myself. I turned, taking in countless directions that looked to be straight shots forward. And every one of them was a trick. Lies that withheld the truth that I needed in order to find my way out.

The lighting dimmed, flickering several times before returning to normal.

As if I wasn't already dealing with enough in this annoyingly never-ending maze, I had to deal with a loss of power. Within seconds, the illumination flashed and weakened, continuing to lose strength.

I slapped at the air, quickening my steps as I sought any open area in the weak lighting. The lights flicked, returning to a dim state. This left me speeding and swiping at hard surfaces and coming face to face with my reflection as the light flicked in ways that awkwardly illuminated my horrified expression.

For far too long, my palms met the cold hard surface and all angles of myself flashed into view. The crowds wouldn't hear yelling, but worse, my pleas for help might draw the brothers' attention if they ventured this way. I didn't want them aware of where I'd trapped myself. But I also didn't want to be left here for an eternity.

I had no choice but to call out and hit the outer sides of my fists against a mirror.

Then came absolute blackness. As though my fight for survival made the power go out. I beat again, going from one mirror to the next, banging.

Another rapid flicker brought a dark form into view. It happened too quickly, but I knew by the height and suave panther-like movement, this was one of the brothers. The villains of my life. The ones who'd led me into this trap as a means of taunting me with impossible escape. But they didn't know me well if they thought I would be the heroine to fall to my knees and submit to their tyranny.

"You weren't actually trying to leave us, were you?"

Puzzlement

*C*aleb. That had to be Caleb. He seemed different, though. Not at all playful in tone.

"Caleb, please." I didn't want to answer his question. He had to have known that I didn't simply come into this maze of horrors to play as his *Little Red*.

He wanted me, though. We meshed perfectly in our love of play. He had no reason to ever help me leave John. Keeping me imprisoned was a win for him as well.

"I can't find my way out," I said.

Another flicker showed him raising a hand to a mirror and sliding his hand along the surface as he moved. "I know the way out."

I turned, looking in all directions to see if I could find him. For the least I knew, he could be around a corner. He could be behind me.

Blackness fell. Not even a step of his could be heard. I had nowhere to go and nothing to do but wait and listen for the quietest tap or for him to speak.

"Caleb," I called.

"Yes, Jules?" His voice came from somewhere to my right. Not in that sultry way he so often spoke to me. This question came out in a tone far more serious than the sweet Caleb I knew.

"Help me out of here," I said, though it came out as more of a beg.

It was in the eerie darkness that I felt his approach, slightly bumping my shoulder. He didn't startle me in the least. I'd hoped he could find me without need of sight.

"What if I don't want to?" he asked, feeling along my lower back before he found his spot behind me and wrapped his arms around me. "You'll only run away and then none of us will get our happily ever after."

At the same time that I felt his lips land against my shoulder, the lights flickered on again, flashing the sight of him behind me. It was a breathtaking sight that didn't last long enough.

But how could I respond to him? Happily ever afters weren't even real. They only occurred in books, and only occasionally were they exceptional.

"You can find someone better than me who you don't have to share with John." It wasn't as though I didn't enjoy Caleb and all the fun he made certain that I would have.

"There's no one better than you, Jules." His mouth trailed to my neck, tickling me with heated breath. "We've already set up a flower shop for you."

They did that for me? So I would stay with them?

"You set up a flower shop?" I attempted a deep inhale, which the tight dress fought allowing.

After a few seconds, crisscrossing strips of crimson on the floor illuminated us, casting many angles of us in a romantic lighting that livened my scarlet dress.

Caleb peeked at our reflection from where he kissed the side of my neck. "John said you wouldn't be happy without one."

All I could do was stare at the two of us. He must have loved the view and kept his sight on me as his hands meandered down my arms.

Guilt pricked at my soul at the realization flowers had been John's thoughtful way to bring me happiness. I'd definitely lowered the dominating man's walls. I'd also insulted and continually rejected him. But what could he expect? He was into sadism and humiliating me. I was into reading about that, not experiencing it.

"I'm sorry, Caleb," I responded. The situation became unbearably painful. Leaving would hurt, but what they planned wasn't the life I wanted.

"I can't tell if you really do want to leave or it's part of your game," he said.

"Game?" I asked, puzzled.

His hold on me tightened. "John got your acceptance. You made clear that we were what you wanted. But..." He let out a frustrated sigh.

Sure, I remembered the meeting with John clearly. He'd said everything he planned to do. And I wanted him to do everything he'd warned me of. And I did agree to any and everything that might come. But I thought that was for the night. For no more than a few hours. Then all the breeding talk came up—

"I'll take you home, if that's what you want." Caleb interrupted my memory of my first encounter with John. I would have given anything to have been fucked by him and lived out a fantasy. A fantasy he tried to give to me long-term.

I covered my mouth, unable to look anywhere in particular and resting my weight against Caleb. They made sure I got what I wanted.

And John detested giving me the abundance of fantasies I craved, but he let me have it, anyway.

"Do you really want to go home, Jules?"

I nodded slowly. "Yes." *And no.*

"I'll lead the way." Caleb stepped around to my right side and took my hand.

He knew the exact steps to take along a maze littered with reflections of us. No matter the angle, we looked perfect together. We looked so right in this silly little carnival exhibit. Most of all, so many glimpses of us seemed to capture John. Despite the age difference, the handsome brothers were so similar to each other.

Guilt weighed down every single step I took over the diagonally lit flooring. It haunted me as though the red light painted me as a ruinous demon come to destroy the lives of the brothers. And that tormented me all the short distance to where Caleb led me out.

To freedom. To my old life...to where I needed books in order to feel life happening.

Once again, the joyful noises of the distant festivities returned. Talking, boisterous laughter, even the low drumming again. And flames that rose with the beat, as though a fire show had begun.

These had been turbulent days. Filled with both fun and angst; unforgettable pleasure and pain. And music. Music far more magnificent than I'd ever heard at any event I'd attended. Music that reminded me of just how beautiful life could be.

My hand felt clammy in Caleb's, and I slowed my steps. Was he upset? He didn't seem to be. Maybe a bit melancholy when he turned to assess why I didn't rush away. But that was what emotional connection did to people. It opened them up to this sort of discontent. Such unhappiness was inevitable when relying upon the presence of someone else for joy.

I refused to look at his handsome yet despairing face. The sooner he took me home, the better. We could get in the Subaru—no, I could take it. I didn't need to spend that much time with Caleb. I'd lose all the courage to leave.

"I want to drive myself home," I said to him. I just needed for him to get me past the crowds and forest, back to the dungeon bus. From there, I could drive myself.

He didn't say anything, but the lack of argument appeared to suggest he would accept the request. But it was a request from someone he didn't actually believe he owned. He'd set it all up. Made it feel so real.

Now I could only step face to face with him, looking up into those enchanting eyes. "Is this a trick?" It had to be a trick. Let it be a trick. Don't let me get away. Don't make me go.

"No, Jules." He shook his head and dug in his pocket, pulling out a set of keys that contained the Subaru key and my purple, flower-shaped house key included.

I reached for the keys, but he pulled them away. "We need to make sure you get home safely." He still offered me a small smile before scanning the crowd in the direction of torches that were being spun into the air.

Once again, I let him lead me onward. To the safety of home and flowers and all my wonderful novels on my tablet. To heroes and antiheroes. The sort of antiheroes that would never let me go, no matter the lengths I might go to escape.

That seemed a bit depressing. Caleb wouldn't even make this a fun parting. It felt too clean. Too...over. As though I'd been swept away into a story that would simply come to a boring ending. Not with a happily ever after, not with a triumphant escape, either. Like the sort of women's fiction novels I would never dare touch.

What would this be? Just walking away with some sort of personal growth. Or worse, just walking away with nothing gained at all.

No matter, that was life. And I had no desire for my life to be the sort of story that inspired wayward souls who wanted to see someone gain some sort of wisdom.

As we continued, the fire became hypnotic, even enchanting. What I would give to be in the midst, experiencing it and imagining all the magnificent things Caleb might do to me. But as I passed, letting it taper into my periphery, it seemed to die. As though I willed an illusion to end and let darkness take hold.

This was the sort of loneliness that took hold in a crowded room of people I had nothing in common with. But this time, I couldn't escape it. I couldn't envision myself somewhere else. All I could do was to cling to Caleb's hand as though it might save me from becoming lost. I couldn't even escape the world around me as I'd always mastered. John and Caleb had changed me. I didn't get to reimagine the world anymore.

But life wasn't done kicking me. It was having too much fun; letting me see a gait that I knew all too well walking across the dark platform. I wouldn't stay. Not for a moment longer. Now I jerked my hand free of Caleb's. I needed to get as far away from this reality as possible.

Then came that wail I knew. The one that only a cello could make. A piece that John knew I loved. That could make me cry. Not that I was overly sensitive. *Canon in D* could make grown men cry throughout the centuries.

And that fucking asshole chose to play it now. The bastard planned to keep me. And, as though he ruled over the masses, the crowd gathered to watch where the stage lit in a low glow of torches. It felt as though a vortex pulled me to him and blocked my struggle to leave with an impenetrable wall of people who'd become enthralled.

I turned to look at the beautiful man who'd magically parted the masses in a way that there was a path to him. More instrumentalists formed a semi-circle behind him, setting up on seats to join in on the melody. And even when they began, not one outshined his ability to capture the soul.

Any woman would become lost in John. They would suffer themselves with the inescapable pain of everything that came with love. The hope of their happily ever after.

He was a sadist. *A sadist.* But my mind and heart battled, disabling me from taking the steps required to leave him and Caleb behind.

When the number ended, his eyes met mine, halting my ability to think. Readjusting his shoulders and letting his fingers find their perfect chord, he slammed the bow onto the strings, releasing a wrathful sound before he led the other musicians to play the angst-filled piece we danced to upon our first meeting. Taunting and inescapable.

But even after all this man had done, I couldn't deny wanting to experience that dance with him time and time and time again.

Final Dance

John laid his instrument down and stood, every bit the doom I knew him to be. He was by far the sexiest man to ever wear such a perfectly fitted black suit. Caleb may have been hot, but he still lacked the mature features that John had developed over a tumultuous thirty-something years.

Every step my way made me want to both melt and run all at the same time. But I couldn't break through the wall of onlookers if I tried. Once again, it felt as though the wolves were on the hunt for me–their Little Red. The one they would always love and torment.

I looked in all directions, knowing I needed my courage to walk away and refuse to remain with him. To not become lost in the same dance we'd shared before he upended my life in a way that I could never feel normal again.

Miraculously, the line of bodies trapping me parted. The couples took hands and began to dance to the powerful music, further complicating my escape with the way they spun and moved. None of them knew the calamity of becoming enthralled by the musicians. Of the eternal loss of self if they so chose to engage in such a dance.

Torches blasted in high flames from the outskirts of this grassy dancefloor. I turned amongst the many people, feeling as though the world spun around me in flames and vibrant colors. A woman twirled from her partner toward where I stepped, causing me to turn and duck beneath the arms of the momentarily parted couple. Then there were other couples in the golden glow of the ethereal flames, pushing from each other before connecting and spinning.

Looking backward, I saw the green eyes that were raised over most heads. And even they were touched by the flames. John was coming for me, and this time he looked more like a demon come to claim me than the first night we danced. And would I let him lead me to the underworld I'd agreed to on that first night he'd set his well-laid trap?

It would be more than a simple taste of the underworld. This would be the unending torments of love. But there would also be joy brought about by the intense man. Joy no one else could ever compare to.

The bodies of the dancers around me slowed with time that seemed to offer me additional seconds to make my decision.

Whether I wanted him or not, I wouldn't stand still in wait. He wouldn't want that, anyway. He may have hated the fantasies I became lost in, but he couldn't deny his love of the chase.

Unwilling to let this be his swift win, I turned, time once again increasing with the beat that had overcome the wills of everyone surrounding me. I found my opening for a quick retreat between couples. A success. At least it would have been until the tune switched. Slower and more lethal. An ancient beat that started with a drumming and matched the torrent of the surrounding flames and had lovers separating, finding strangers and taking hands, pushing and pulling, spinning with urgency.

I came face to face with a man, no one remarkable, just a man who took my hands and pulled me to him. We spun, me catching sight of John, who'd shifted his prowl to circle around the many bodies that had come between us.

I spun, breaking free of this man, already on the search of my next move. Before I could bolt further, I came face to face with Caleb, who raised his hand in offer.

I twirled away from the younger brother, my back landing against someone else. A short man whose arm wrapped around me. He gripped my hand and pulled, sending me outward in a twirl I fought free of, leaving me unwound within inches of John's harsh expression.

Without missing a single beat, John's strong arms shot out, grabbing me at my waist and pulling me so our bodies collided.

"You're going to dance with me." He didn't even bother with asking, just as he hadn't upon our first meeting. A brooding man I no longer wanted to oppose. And unlike our meeting, I found my footing instantly, keeping up with his movements, turning as he turned, my eyes magnetically drawn to his fiendish gaze that stared downward with dominance.

"I'm going to fuck you," he warned, even more enticing than the same promise during the dance we'd shared.

We spun together; him bringing me so close, his chin almost bumped my brow. His voice seemed both lethal and alluring. "And I'm not going to take no for an answer." Just as our first night, he possessively held me with his fingertips firm to my lower back.

And I knew just how many wonderful things those fingers of his could do. I could tell he read into my desire for this dance to continue. He knew my longing to learn more of his plans for me. But this time, I couldn't rely on fantasy. Our future would be real.

He stepped backward, keeping his firm control over me as well. "You'll try to fight me."

So what if I wanted to? I had every right to demand this be just as fun for me as it was for him. And it was fun for him. He'd set our adventure up, after all.

"I'll always overpower you." His delight made evident that I was his, irrevocably and completely. He wanted *me*. This *me* in his arms, who hung onto his every word with hope.

I wanted him to do anything and everything to me. *Him*. Not the fantasy, but the man before me. The man who'd wanted me since before we met. A man who saw what my needs were and who'd willingly met me on middle-ground.

"Rip off my dress?" I asked, continuing the conversation from our first dance when he'd had me ready to throw out all morals and reasoning to spend a night in a bed with him.

He brought me closer, prodding my stomach with his erection. "You know me too well, Julie."

The beat slowed but remained menacing, and he raised my arm to slowly twirl me until my back rested against his chest.

I spotted Caleb weaving his way around a couple dancing in front of me. He also narrowed in on me.

John's lips tickled my right ear as he spoke. "I'm going to restrain you in a way you'll never escape me."

The thought of being locked away in his dungeon excited me in a way I could no longer deny. Yet again, he would make certain I almost couldn't escape.

I breathed the next words I knew were to come. "Ravish me without mercy?"

And just as the night we met, I would gladly accept any amount of torment to be in his clutches—no, in both of the brothers' clutches.

He hummed against my right ear. "Forever," he promised me.

The depth of his voice added to the ache building in my core. I turned in his hold, my body tight to his as I faced him. "Okay."

"Then you accept?" He spoke the words so much more affectionately than the first night. His green eyes bounced between mine as he gaged my response.

This time, I accepted his every promise, no matter where we might end up. "Yes," I replied, raising onto the tips of my toes to kiss the handsome man whose face tilted to mine.

I hadn't thought I could be squeezed any tighter, but his arms further wrapped around me as he took control of the impassioned connection we shared. It was a hold I melted into long after the kiss while I remained locked against him as bodies danced and torches blazed in the periphery.

His mesmerizing gaze flicked past me, then to me again, and he loosened his arms. I already knew what he'd seen. Caleb. The sweet younger brother wanted his dance as well.

I raised on my toes to kiss John again before his hold on me waned. I then turned to find Caleb awaiting me. His lower lip tucked between his teeth in a coy smile as he raised his hand for me to take. Before I could raise mine, John's splayed hand landed on my stomach and pulled me so my back was to his chest.

I only looked onward to Caleb's extended hand as John's palm moved down my corseted middle, continuing to the frilly skirt. The first night, his fingers met panties, but now, as they meandered between my legs, they landed upon my drenched core.

I couldn't fear him discovering my desire to be his and Caleb's. He already knew. He'd always known that he was what I desperately craved and needed. And now, he reminded me he knew.

He thrummed that spot between my legs as his words tickled my ear. "Go ahead and play, Julie. But you're still going to be punished for trying to escape me."

"Okay," I breathed the silly word of agreement I always had. But I knew it wasn't punishment I would receive later.

Caleb grinned, taking my raised hand and pulling me into his arms. "You almost had me worried you didn't believe in happy endings, Jules."

"I do now." I replied, matching his beaming grin that reached his sea-green eyes.

HEA

It wasn't hard to get Caleb to agree to a springtime trip cross-country to get to a super-bloom and the festival I'd been contracted to decorate. John, on the other hand, didn't like being that far away from doctors and modern comforts. The only way he agreed to this adventure included replacing the dungeon with a fully functioning kitchen, amongst other homey comforts.

The kitchen was definitely a good upgrade, because the pasta covered with alfredo and broccoli that John carried out to me smelled divine. He set it down on the windowsill to the bright yellow wooden caravan wagon and grabbed the vase of pink and white blooms from my hold. His eyes narrowed. "That weighs more than ten pounds!"

"It's less than twenty." I was only five months pregnant and could lift more than that much weight without doctors complaining. I let out a long, exaggerated breath and released the vase for him to take. He carefully clutched it and climbed into the wagon, crouching as he went to the far corner and set down the vase of light pink carnations. He then pulled a short table from beneath the twin-sized bed, got the plate of pasta and set it on the table. His eyebrows rose with his demanding stare that suggested I come to eat. I may have acted annoyed with his dedication to my wellbeing once we learned we were expecting, but he knew I loved how much he cared about mine and the baby's health.

I climbed the few steps into the small wagon and sat on the floor where the plate heaped with my favorite meal waited in front of me. This past year was more perfect than what I could ever have expected my life to be. Two wonderful men, a baby girl on the way, and a flower shop that received orders from locations coast to coast.

And this festival that a mystery client hired me to decorate was based on a steamy romance about a wayward human who'd been kidnapped from earth and traveled the forests of Faerie by two Fae princes with a mobile wagon dungeon. I thought it was a pretty good book. So did Caleb. And even John did once I softened the more dominating prince. They even gave it five-star ratings. The only ratings it received, and they were likely the only readers.

I lifted the plate and rapidly scooped forkfuls into my mouth, realizing how ravenous I'd become. Most of the way through the meal, as I spun noodles on the fork, I caught John's hungry stare.

"Stop it," I said, blushing and unable to control my grin. I loved everything that happened whenever he became so watchful.

One of his eyebrows raised. "Stop what?" he asked. His gaze flared with lust, much like the dominating Fae prince in the novel.

"Caleb might come back and see us." I enjoyed both men, but there was no small amount of rivalry between them when it came to my pleasure.

I tried to focus my attention on the rest of my food, pretending to ignore John's sexual hunger that had me ready to submit to him on the small bed.

"He won't be back for another forty minutes, and I *might* let him have a turn with you then." John stooped toward the door, closed it, and set the little wooden bar that locked it. He came over to sit on the floor beside me. "Happy now?" he asked, leaning against my side to plant kisses along my neck.

I twirled one of the last bites of pasta around the fork, failing to ignore the warmth that had an ache forming between my legs. I loved everything about this man; about both of the men who claimed me. And their touch felt even more electrical these last few months as my sex-drive and connection to them increased exponentially by the day.

"Don't stop eating..." John ordered, twisting so he could pull my long skirt upward and find that sensitive spot at my core, strumming me to a very blissful release. "Or I'll have to punish you."

He'd given me no option but to lower the plate to see what he had in store for me for the next forty minutes. And I was sure to love every moment.

Milton Keynes UK
Ingram Content Group UK Ltd.
UKHW022052260924
448786UK00012B/506